101 PANCHATANTRA TALES (ILLUSTRATED)

BY PANDIT VISHNU SHARMAN

EDITED & ILLUSTRATED BY VYANST

101 Panchatantra Tales (Illustrated)
By Pandit Vishnu Sharman
Edited and Illustrated by Vyanst
Copyright © 2015 Vyanst

PREFACE

Panchatantra is an integral part of classic Indian literature. The stories of Panchatantra were first narrated by Pandit Vishnu Sharman, who was hired as a tutor to teach the three witless sons of King Amarashakti. It is said that the powerful messages in these stories drastically improved the three princes' who went on to become efficient rulers in future. The tales provide valuable lessons of life and are deemed essential in the development of a child. The different states and languages in India have added their own flavors to enrich these tales. Panchatantra, is now a timeless classic for its allegorical tales and is popular all over the world as a guide in solving problems of life.

The word Panchatantra is derived from "Pancha" which means five and "Tantra" which means strategies. Pandit Vishnu Sharman devised his stories based on five strategies.
The five strategies are:

First Strategy: The Gaining of Friends
Second Strategy: Discord among Friends
Third Strategy: Of Crows and Owls
Fourth Strategy: Loss of Gains
Fifth Strategy: Imprudence

TABLE OF CONTENTS

1. The Tailor and the Elephant

Long, long ago, there lived a big elephant in a small town. Despite his enormous physique, he was a very loving creature. People loved him and offered him delicious fruits to eat.

While going to river to take a bath regularly he passed a tailor's shop. The tailor always gave him something to eat. The two became friends.

As usual one day, the elephant put his trunk inside the shop. The tailor decided to play a prank on him. The tailor instead of giving him something to eat pricked a needle into his trunk. The elephant writhed in pain and sat on the ground. Some people gathered around him and began to laugh.

Although, the elephant was angry, he quietly went away.

One day, the tailor's son went to the river with his friends. While playing he suddenly slipped into the river and fell into it. He started screaming for help. The elephant, who was at the river for his bath, saw the child in distress and immediately rescued him. The tailor regretted his earlier behavior and thanked the elephant. He vowed to never again play a mischievous prank that hurts others.

Moral : Do not hurt others.

2. The Rat with Four Tails

Once there was a small rat who was born with four tails. He had no friends and often used to roam the streets. One day he saw a group of children playing in a park. Being curious he went near the kids. As soon as the children saw him, they began to mock him, "Look at that funny rat with four tails!", they laughed.

The little rat was deeply hurt and he went home and cut one of his tails. Next day he went to the park again. The children again mocked him for his three tails. He again went home and cut one tail. Now the children mocked him for his two tails, so finally he cut one more tail.

Now the rat was sure that he was just an ordinary rat with one tail and no one will mock him. But alas, he was so wrong for the children again laughed at him. "Look at that rat with an ugly tail!", they said.

The little rat went home and cut his final tail, "Now no one will tease me!", he thought.

But the next day when he went near the children, they mocked, "Look at the funny rat, he has no tail!"

The little rat now repented for acting in a haste and losing all his tails.

Moral : Do not give undue importance to someone's mocking and act in a haste.

3. The Cap Seller and the Monkeys

Once, there was a cap-seller in a small town. One fine day, he was selling caps, in the town, "Caps! caps! caps! Buy now! Nice colorful caps!"

He roamed around for a while and sold some caps. It was a hot summer day and he soon became tired. He decided to lie down under the shade of a big banyan tree and take rest for a while. Soon, he slept off.

Meanwhile, there were some monkeys sitting on the top of the tree. They saw the cap-seller and the colorful basket of caps. The curious monkeys came down, took the caps out from the cap-seller's basket and wore them. Then they climbed the tree again.

When the cap seller woke up, he was shocked to see his basket empty. He searched for his caps. To his surprise, when he looked up, he saw the monkeys were wearing his caps. He took a stone and hurled at the monkeys. The stone missed its mark. But the monkeys too shot him back with the fruits on the tree.

The cap seller soon realized that the monkeys imitated his actions. So he smartly removed his own cap and threw it down. And how right he was! The monkeys just imitated and removed the caps and threw them down. The cap-seller smiled at his own little wise plan and gathered all the caps on the ground, put them in his basket and quickly went away.

Moral : A clever person will always find a way out of a problem.

4. The Two Parrots

Once a hunter caught two parrots from the nest of a tree. One of the parrots escaped from the hands of the hunter, flew and took shelter in a hermitage. One parrot was brought up by the hunter in his hut and the other in the hermitage of the sage.

One day the king of the country approached the hut of the hunter to quench his thick tired after hunting. The parrot with the hunter cried:

"An intuder...An intruder...Catch him...Catch him..."

The scared king went away. He approached the hermitage. The parrot there with a soft voice said.

"O respected guest, Welcome to you, Welcome to you. Have you thirst quenched. Be our guest for the lunch!"

The sage came out and welcomed the king wide all reverence to the guest.

The king asked the sage:

"O sage : How is that the two parrots born to the same parents have behaved quite differently, one rudely and the other so nicely?

The sage replied:

"O king, the behavior of any person depends on the environment in which he is brought up. The other parrot is being brought up by a hunter who is by nature rude and cruel. This other parrot is brought up by us, the sages. Hence the difference in their behavior.

Moral : One's behavior is based upon the environment in which he/she is brought up .

5. The Thirsty Crow

Long ago, there lived a crow in a jungle. Once he was wandering in search of water to quench his thirst. At last, he came flying over a village. There he saw a pitcher lying in front of a house. There was some water in it. The crow tried to reach the water, but couldn't succeed. The water level was too low in the pitcher. The crow began to think of some practicable device and finally came up with a bright idea. He looked around and found a pebble. He picked up the pebble in his beak and dropped it into the pitcher.

The crow realized that the water level had risen a little. So he dropped more pebbles in the pitcher till the water level was high enough for his beak to touch it. The thirsty crow then drank the water to his hearts content and flew away.

Moral : Necessity is the mother of invention.

6. The Two Enemies

Once upon a time, there was a huge mountain range, where sages named Kasha and Kama conducted penance. Though they lead a saintly life, they always fought with one another and never lived a moment of peace. They were sworn enemies.

Sometimes, they even postponed their prayers only to argue with one another. One year there was huge scarcity of food in that region. One fine day, other sages who lived there decided to move away from that place, the first reason being scarcity of food and the next being, the never ending nuisance created by Kacha and Kama. Irritated by their behaviour, when the others moved away, instead of learning from their mistakes, both of them again fought blaming each other for the exit of sages.

This time the argument touched new heights and there was a huge ego clash. "I shall please the Lord and see that this place has no scarcity of food again," vowed Kacha.

"Before you can do that, I Shall please the Lord and ensure that there is abundant water here", vowed Kama.

Both of them thus challenged each other, turned towards two different hilltops and started penance. They continued to pray for the Lord for several years not bothered about anything else in the world. Finally, pleased with them, the Lord decided to bless them with whatever they asked for.

He first appeared before Kacha and told him to ask whatever he wanted. Kacha thought for a while and asked," Oh Lord! Even Kama had been praying for you since many years. Have you visited him?"

Lord Almighty replied,"No Kacha! I have come to you first I would visit Kama after blessing you with whatever you want."

"Then Lord! Please bless me the double of whatever Kama asks for." Was the instant answer from Kacha.

"So be it!" Said the Lord and appeared before Kama who was on the Other hill. He blessed Kama and told him to ask for boon of his choice.

Kama was too pleased to see the Lord in front of him. His joy knew no bounds. But after a few seconds, he had a doubt in his mind. He bowed to Lord Almighty and asked, "Oh Lord! Have you come to me first or have you already visited Kacha?"

When the Lord replied that he had already visited Kacha, Kama could not control his anxiety and inquired what Kacha had asked for. Lord Almighty smiled and narrated the discussion between HIM and Kacha.

Then Kama thought for a while and said, "Oh Lord! If that's the case, then please make me blind in one eye, That is what I want from you."

Immediately, Lord Almighty granted his boon and disappeared from there. Soon after the Lord disappeared, Kama lost one eye and Kacha lost both his eyes. Later both met one another and repented for their haste that resulted in loss of vision.

Realizing that they landed in such a condition only because of their ego and enimity, they went to the other sages and begged for pardon. Since then, they stopped fighting and started serving others with pure hearts. After a few years, pleased by the difference in their behaviour Lord Almighty again appeared before them and restored their vision. That was the moment when Kacha & Kama truly realized that 'Good deeds will yield good results'.

Moral : Think before you act.

7. The Wise Tree

One day, all the animals of a forest gathered together to have a meeting, They all spoke and discussed many things. Though initially, the meeting was fun, by the end of it, they all started arguing and fighting with one another trying to prove their superiority.

"I am great" said an animal and another said, "No! I am great." This situation continued for a while. Suddenly, the Lion roared and said, "Since I am ferocious, strong and also the King of the jungle,I am superior."

"No! That is not true. I am huge and my tusks are precious. Humans pay huge amounts to buy them. Thats why I am great." Said the elephant.

"Stop it! I am greater than all of you." Roared the tiger.

The tree which was standing there, broke in to peels of laughter all of a sudden. Irritated by the tree, the animals asked why it was laughing .

The tree said, "Your argument is very amusing, Actually, I am greater than all of you."

Now it was the tiger's turn to laugh. He said, "You can't stand a storm, your leaves fall off when there is a strong breeze and above all, humans axe you and chop you with ease. How can you say you are superior to all of us?"

"Think carefully. I give shelter to animals and birds. My leaves provide oxygen to all of you, to breathe. I give the humans, shelter and also my fruits. I am useful for cooking too. So I am, no doubt the best." Replied the tree. All the animals agreed to its logic and nodded in agreement.

Then, the tree again said, "Friends! Not only me, but also every creation of God is unique in its own way. Every thing has it's own advantages. Hence, we are all equally great." All the animals realized their mistakes and thanked the tree for enlightening them.

Moral : Each of us are unique and all are equal in God's eyes.

8. The Kind Hearted Tiger

One day, a tiger was starving of hunger. Through he roamed in the entire forest, he couldn't get any thing to eat. "Why am I suffering like this today? Why am I unable to find any food in his forest? Where did all animals go?", thought he helplessly.

In the meanwhile, he saw a cow that was grazing in the fields nearby. His joy knew no bounds. He quickly ran towards the cow to kill it. The cow noticed the tiger and started shivering with fear. She fell down on her knees before the tiger and pleaded him to spare her life.

"Oh Tiger! I have small child, whom I should look after. If you kill me now, my child would be orphaned", cried the cow.

The tiger was unmoved by her words. "Hey you! I am hungry today. None of your words are going to stop me from killing you", roared the tiger.

When the cow knew that her death was inevitable, she said, "I won't stop you, if you want kill me. But I have not gone home since morning. My child must be waiting for me. Please give me a chance to give him milk and say good bye. Then, you can kill me as you please."

The tiger agreed to the cows plea and followed the cow to her shed. As soon as the calf saw his mother, he came running to her and embraced her tightly. The cow too kissed her child and gave him milk. When the tiger saw them, he was moved. "There would be no greatness in separating this mother and child," thought the tiger.

He than went to the cow and said, "Oh cow! I have changed my mind . I won't kill you. Please live happily with your child."

Saying so, the tiger turned back and went towards the forest. The cow thanked the kind-hearted tiger for sparing her life.

Moral : A mother's love can move a mountain.

9. Self Help

Once upon a time, there was a sparrow that lived in a wheat field with her children. One day a farmer, the owner of the field came there to check the growth of the crop. Extremely elated to see his ripe field, almost ready for harvest, he thought,"Well! it is time to cut the crop. I shall call my friends and relatives to help me in harvesting."

The young sparrows heard the farmers words and at once knew that their nest would soon be destroyed. Frightened to the core, they waited for their mother to return in the evening. As soon as the mother sparrow came home, they circled her and said, "Mother! There is a bad news for us. The owner of this field is going to harvest this field with the help of his friends and relatives, tomorrow."

The mother sparrow smiled and said, "Have no fears my children! The time to leave this nest has not come yet. The farmer is thinking of seeking help from others, which will not come. Remember, one who depends on others for his work can never finish it." As anticipated by the mother sparrow, though the farmer waited for his people to come, but none had turned up.

A few days after, the farmer again visited the field and found that the Head was overflowing with ripe crop. "I sought the help of my relatives and friends but none of them came. Since, the field is full, I shall get some laborers and harvest the crop before it is destroyed, instead of relying on others.", said the farmer to himself, which the young sparrows over heard. The young ones again waited for their mothers return and narrated the day's incidents to their mother.

This time, the mother sparrow did not advise her kids to relax. Instead, she said, "Kids! it's time to leave this nest. The farmer really intends to harvest his crop on his own." Saying so, the mother sparrow took her children and flew away to another place.

Moral : Self - help is the best help

10. The Lion and the Cows

Long, long ago, there lived four cows in a jungle. They were best friends. They always grazed together and saved each other when some wild animal attacked them. This was the reason why even tigers and lions couldn't gather the courage to kill and eat them .A lion had, indeed, an eye upon these cows. But he could never find the right opportunity to make them his prey.

One day, the cows fell out. Each one grazed separately her own way. This was the right opportunity for the lion to attack them. So, the lion hid himself behind the bushes and when a lonely cow would come closer to the bushes, he would pounce upon her and kill her for his meals. In this way, all the four cows were killed one by one by the lion.

Moral : Unity is strength.

11. The Donkey in the grab of Tiger's skin

There was a washerman by name Shuddhapata in a village near Pataliputra. He had a donkey. It had become very feeble from lack of fodder as its food. The washerman one day found a dead tiger on the forest. He thought "I will put this tiger skin on the donkey. The farmers will think the donkey as a tiger and will not drive it out".

When this was done, the donkey ate barley to his heart's content. The donkey grew stout. One day the donkey heard the bray of a female donkey in the distance. As was his habit, it also began to bray. Then the farmers found out that it was only a donkey in disguise. They then killed the donkey with blows from clubs and stones and arrows.

Moral : A fake disguise cannot hide natural instincts.

12. The Clever Doves

There was a huge banyan tree standing on the outer boundaries of a village. All kinds of birds had their homes in this tree. Even the travelers would come and relax under its cool shade during the hot summer days.

Once, a fowler set his net under the tree and strewed some grains of rice to lure the birds. A crow living in the tree saw it and cautioned his friends not to go down to eat the rice.

But at the same moment, a flock of doves came flying over the banyan tree. They saw grains of rice strewn around and without losing a moment, descended on the ground to eat the grains of rice. As soon as they started eating the rice, a huge net fell over them and they were all trapped. They tried everything to come out of the net, but in vain. They saw the fowler coming towards them. He was very happy to find a large number of doves trapped inside the net.

However, the king of doves was very intelligent and clever. He said to other doves, "We must do something immediately to free ourselves from the clutches of this fowler. I've an idea. We should all fly up together clutching the net in our beaks. We will take it to our friend, the mouse, to request him to tear the net with his sharp teeth and set us free. Now, come on friends, let's fly."

So each dove picked up a part of the huge net in his beak and they all flew up together. Seeing the birds flying along with the whole net, the fowler was surprised. He could never imagine this. He ran after the flying birds, shouting madly, but could not catch them. Soon the birds flew out of his sight and reached the mouse.

The mouse praised the king dove for his intelligence and nibbled at the portion of the net, which would set free the doves..All the doves were very grateful to the mouse. They thanked the mouse and then flew to their destination happily.

Moral : Unity is strength

13. The Fox and the Tortoise

One day, a starving fox captured a tortoise, but it could not manage to break through the solid shell in order to eat it.

'You should drop me in the water for a while to soften me up,' suggested the shrewd tortoise.

"But if I drop you in water, you will run away", the fox worried.

The tortoise then devised a plan. He said, "Why don't you sit on my shell and I will carry you down the river. The river water will soften me up and then you can eat me."

The fox liked this plan and he sat on the tortoise's back. Half way through the river, the fox asked, "I guess you should have softened up now. Let's go to the bank".

The tortoise replied,"Yes, I am almost soft at all areas except where you are sitting. Can you move aside so that I can soften that area too and then you can eat me."

The greedy fox did not think twice and moved aside only to fall into the river. The fox drowned soon and the tortoise escaped.

Moral : With wits and intelligence, one can defeat a mighty enemy.

14. The Two Cats

One day a little bird was resting on a small log. Suddenly two cats came from opposite sides of the log. Both the cats wanted to have the little bird for themselves. Each of them refused to back out and started to quarrel. The little bird was sleeping peacefully unaware of the ruckus.

After fighting for sometime, the cats decided to pounce on the bird. Just then the little bird got up and flew away and the two cats bumped and crashed their heads against each other. The cats had to go home empty-handed.

Moral : A third person benefits from a quarrel between two.

15. Who is the Greatest?

One day, an argument broke out amongst all the animals in the forest. They were debating on who was the greatest of them. The lion said, "I am the mightiest and everyone calls me the king of the jungle. Obviously I am the greatest animal."

The deer replied, "I run fastest and hence I am the greatest animal."

The lion roared, "O deer! How dare you compare yourself to me? It seems you do not value your life. I will make you my prey today". Saying so, he ran behind the deer.

The butterfly said, "I go across flower to flower and plant seeds. Without me there would not have been this forrest, hence I am the greatest".

"I am the best dancer with no one to compete with me. Hence I am the greatest", remarked the peacock.

"My sweet voice enchants everyone, hence it is only me who is the greatest", retorted the cuckoo.

Thus they kept arguing and fighting. No one was listening to the other. The Vanadevata (Goddess of the forest) was listening to this commotion. She appeared in front of all the animals and said, "Each of you has a unique quality and greatness of its own. You must stop fighting and stay together as friends to make this forest a wonderful place."

The animals realized their mistake and apologized to the goddess.

Moral : We must appreciate the fact that each person is unique.

16. The Farmer and his Lazy Sons

There lived a very hardworking farmer, named Gopal, in a village. He had five sons. All of them were strong and healthy. But they were all lazy.

The farmer was sad thinking about his sons and the future of his farmland. One day, he got a flash of an idea. He called all his sons and said, "Dear sons! I have hidden a treasure in our farmland. You search and share the treasure among you."

The five sons were overjoyed. They went to the fields and started searching. They dug each and every inch of the field. But they could not find anything.

Gopal said to his sons, "Dear boys! Now you have tooled and conditioned the field, why not we sow a crop!" Off went the sons to sow the crops.

Days passed. Soon, the crops grew lushly green. The sons were delighted. The father said, "Sons, this is the real treasure I wanted you to share".

Moral : God Almighty always has a way to punish a person who does evil to others.

17. The Sour Grapes

A fox was starving for days as all his attempts to get food did not bear any results. Wandering in search of something to eat, he chanced upon a vineyard. There were large bunches of golden grapes hung from the vines above his head.

The fox jumped up and down, trying to bite into a bunch of the grapes, but he fell short. He tried again and again with all his might, but he still failed to reach the grapes.

Tired and defeated he decided to quit, but consoled himself, as well as he could, by telling himself, "It doesn't matter, because grapes were ripe, but I see now they are quite sour."

It was the fox's typical nature to blame the grapes for his failure.

Moral : You cannot hide your failure with a lame excuse.

18. The Frog and the King

One day the king of Panchal, Rajendra, was walking in his royal garden, enjoying the nature. While walking he came to a pond that had many frogs in it. The king of frogs was sitting on a rock, in the middle of the pond. When he saw the Panchal king, the frog king said, "Who are you? How dare you come to my territory?"

"I am Rajendra, the king of this region of Panchal. Who are you?", replied the amused king Rajendra.

"O! You might be the king of this region, but I am the king of frogs. I am better than you as I have many qualities that you do not have", boasted the frog king.

"Please tell me your qualities", asked king Rajendra.

"You walk very slow, but I can cover a great distance with just one hop and leap. I am a great singer, Can you croak like me?", replied the frog king.

"O Frog king!", replied king Rajendra, "The hopping and croaking are your inherent qualities that God gave you. God made all of us different with our own unique qualities. I can never hop or croak like you, just as you can never do things like human."

The frog king understood his mistake and apologized for his behavior.

Moral : God gave inherent and unique qualities to each being in this Universe.

19. The Humming bird and the Crow

Once, a Humming bird and a crow lived on a tree. They wanted to go on a pilgrimage. They went to the sea to see the God Garuda (Eagle-god). On the way they saw a shepherd. He was carrying a pot full of curd. The crow flying on to the pot was eating the curd frequently. The shepherd noticed it. He removed the pot from his head and kept it down on the ground. He looked up. He saw both the birds. The Humming bird which could not fly as fast as the crow was caught by the shepherd and killed.

The Humming bird, which was a good one suffered, because it was in a bad company.

Moral : Stay away from bad company.

20. The Greatness of a Rose

In a beautiful garden there were Marigold and Rose flowers.

One day the Marigold said to the Rose :

"My dear Rose friend ! You look very beautiful! Many people like you very much. Your appearance, your color, your smell gives happiness to everyone around you. People offer you to God while they pray."

Listening to these words rose sighed, "But my life span is very short. Even when people don't pluck me, my petals fall off the next day."

Many people live for a very long time, even though they do nothing for the society. Some people who though stay for a short period serve the society. They will be remembered forever. Rose belongs to that category.

Moral : A life, even if it is short, is served best in the service of others.

21. The Couple Who Fought

There lived a poor woodcutter named Murali in a small village. He and his wife, Radha, used to always bicker and fight. One day Murali got some wheat flour and asked Radha to make two roti's for dinner, one roti for each of them. However there was bit more flour and she ended up making three roti's. Now the couple started to fight over who will eat the extra roti.

Radha said, "I made the roti and hence it should be mine."

Murali replied, "Had I not bought the flour you would not have made these roti's in the first place. Hence it is only fair that I get the extra roti."

Thus they continued their argument and fought hard. Finally they decided not to eat any roti's until the other person backed off. They sat for a while and did not know when they fell asleep.

Meanwhile, seeing the door open, a street dog entered the house. The dog saw the three roti's on the plate. It quickly took the roti's and ran away.

Moral : A third person always benefits by a fight between two people.

22. The Tortoise and the Scorpion

Once, a tortoise and a scorpion were friends. One day the scorpion wanted to go to the other side of the river. The scorpion, being a very poor swimmer, asked the tortoise to carry him on his back across the river. The tortoise agreed to carry him on his back.

The scorpion climbed aboard, but halfway across the river the scorpion gave the turtle a mighty sting. The shell protected the tortoise but he was unhappy and asked, "Why did you sting me? Aren't you my friend?"

The scorpion replied, "It is just my character to sting."

The tortoise said, "Ok then it is my character to swim deep below the surface of this river." Saying so he went down the river and drowned the scorpion.

Moral : Stay away from evil friends.

23. The Honest Wood-cutter

Ramu was a poor man. He earned his living by cutting wood and selling it. He had a big family to support.

One day, when Ramu went into the forest to cut wood, he slipped off and his axe went down into a nearby well. He tired his best, but he could not get back his axe. He started weeping.

Suddenly Ramu heard a voice calling,"Ramu! What is your problem?"

He lifted his head and saw a fairy in front of him. He told, "I lost my axe in the well."

The fairy said, "Don't worry, I will get you your axe."

Saying this, the fairy dived into the pond. The fairy came up with a golden axe decorated with precious stones and asked, "Ramu, is this the axe?"

Ramu said, "No."

The fairy dived once more. This time, the fairy came up with a silver axe. Once again Ramu said, "No, this is not mine".

The third time the fairy came up with Ramu's axe. Now, Ramu was filled with joy.

The fairy too was happy at Ramu's honesty. She gave Ramu all the three axes and blessed him.

Moral : Honesty Pays.

24. The Clever Rabbit

In a forest, there was a cruel lion, which used to kill all the animals he saw. He was so wicked that the animals were scared to move freely in the forest. One day, the hungry lion was roaming in search of food. Exactly then, he saw a little rabbit. Though the rabbit tried to escape, the lion obstructed it's way and said, "You little one! I have been hungry since yesterday. Now I am going to kill you and satisfy my hunger."

Shivering with fear, the rabbit pleaded the lion to leave him. "Sir! I am too small an animal to satisfy your hunger. Please leave me.", he cried.

But the lion refused to listen. "I shall first eat you and then kill some other animal too" he replied and got ready pounce on him.

Then, a brilliant idea flashed in the rabbit's mind. He suddenly fell on the ground and started rolling fiercely. "What happened?" asked the surprised lion.

"My Lord! I have just eaten some leaves from the near by bush. It seems some snake had spit its poison on them. Thats why I am suffering from this unbearable pain. If you eat me, I am sure the poison is going to kill you too. But anyway, if you die, at least the other animals will be freed from you." Said the rabbit acting as if it was going to die.

The lion was shocked when he heard the rabbit's words. "I don't want to invite my death by eating you." Said the lion and ran away from there. The rabbit smiled at the lions foolishness and went away from there feeling glad to be alive.

Moral : One can save himself in a tricky situation using his wits.

25. The Greedy Barber

Choodamani, who was the king of Ayodhya wanted have a lot of money. So he prayed to Lord Siva. Lord Siva asked Kubera, the God of wealth to appear in the dream of Choodamani. Kubera appeared in his dream and told him, "Get up in the morning. Have a shave. Take a stout stick, stand infront of your house. Hit on the head of the first beggar who comes. The beggar will get transformed into a gold vessel".

The king amassed a lot of money by doing as Kubera told him in the dream.

A barber came to know this. He also got shaved, took a stout stick, stood in front of his house and hit the first beggar who came there. The beggar died without changing into a gold vessel. The king imposed death sentence on the foolish barber.

Moral : Do not imitate others foolishly.

26. The Blue Jackal

There lived a jackal named Chandarava in a jungle. One day, he hadn't eaten anything since morning and was so hungry that he wandered and wandered across the jungle, but couldn't find anything to eat. He thought it better to walk a little further and find something to eat in some village. He reached a nearby small village. There on its outskirts he ate some food, but the quantity was not sufficient and he was still very hungry. Then he entered another village with the hope of getting some more food.

As soon as the jackal entered the village, a few dogs charged at him, barking loudly. The jackal was terribly frightened. He began running through lanes in order to save himself from the dogs. Soon he saw a house. The door of the house was open. It was a washerman's house.'This is the right place for me to hide', the jackal thought to himself and ran through the open door.

While trying to hide himself, the jackal slipped and fell into a tank full of blue color, which the washerman had kept ready to dye the clothes.

Soon the barking of the dogs ceased. The jackal saw them going away. He came out of the tub. There was a big mirror fixed on the wall of a room. There was no one around. The jackal entered the room and saw his image in the mirror. He was surprised to see his color. He looked blue. He came out of the house and ran back to the jungle.

When the animals of the jungle saw the blue jackal they were frightened. They had never seen such an animal. Even the lions and tigers were no exceptions. They too were scared of the seemingly strange animal.

The jackal was quick to realize the change in the behavior of the other animals. He decided to take advantage of this funny situation.

"Dear friends", said the blue jackal, "don't be afraid of me. I'm your well-wisher. Lord Brahma has sent me to look after your well-being. He has appointed me as your king."

All the animals of the jungle developed unshakable faith in the blue jackal and accepted him as their king. They brought presents for him and obeyed his commands. The blue jackal appointed the lion as his commander-in-chief; the wolf was appointed the defense minister and the elephant the home minister.

Thus, the blue jackal began living in luxury with the lions and tigers also at his command. What to talk of the smaller animals?

The tigers and leopards brought him delicious food everyday.The blue jackal now was ruling the jungle. He used to hold daily court. All the animals were like his servants. Even the lion hunted small animals and gave them to the blue jackal to eat.

Once, when the blue jackal was holding his famous court, he heard a pack of jackals howling outside his palace. Those jackals had come from some other jungle and were howling, singing and dancing. The blue jackal forgot that he was a king and not an ordinary jackal any more. Instinctively, he too began howling, singing and dancing. All the animals were surprised to see their king howling like a jackal. Soon the word spread around that their king was simply a jackal and not a representative of Lord Brahma. He had fooled the animals. All the animals, in a fit of rage, killed the blue jackal immediately.

Moral : A cheater is always caught.

27. Monkey and the Two Cats

It was the aftermath of a big festival. Two cats were prowling together. One of the cats saw a big cake and meowed. The other jumped up and picked it.

The first cat said, "Give me the cake. It is I who saw it first."

The other cat said "Keep away from it. It is I who picked it up."

They were fighting and fighting. But there was no solution. Just then, a monkey passed by. He thought "What foolish cats they must be! Let me make use of this chance."

He came to the cats and said in a loud voice. "Don't fight. Let me share the cake among you both". The cake was handed over to the monkey.

The monkey split the cake into two parts. He shook his head and said, "Oh! One is bigger. One is smaller". He had a bit of the bigger and now said "Oh! This has become smaller now". He ate from the other. And thus, he went on eating from part to part and finally finished the whole cake.

The poor cats were disappointed.

Moral : When you quarrel someone else gains.

28. The Fox and the Donkey

A river flew through a forest on the outskirts of a village. One day, a hungry fox came to quench his thirst at the river. As he was drinking water, he saw a donkey drinking water on the other bank.

The fox thought, "I know that all donkeys are fools. It will be very easy for me to catch this animal for my lunch."

So the fox said, "Hey Donkey, I have heard that you are a famous singer. Can you please sing a song for me?"

The donkey was happy to hear his praise from the fox.

"Sure sir, Let me sing for you," the foolish donkey said. He lifted his head up to the sky, closed his eyes and started braying. The fox crossed over the bridge and caught the donkey when he was braying.

But the donkey was clever.

He said, "Oh Sir! Do you want to eat me? It will be an honor to be your food, but I have heard that good foxes pray to God before the lunch. Is it not true?"

"Yes, yes, I must pray before lunch," said the fox and closed his eyes to pray. The donkey kicked the fox hard and ran away.

Moral : Wits can save you from difficult situation.

29. The Fox and the Crow

One bright morning as the Fox was following his sharp nose through the wood in search of a bite to eat, he saw a Crow on the limb of a tree overhead. This was by no means the first Crow the Fox had ever seen. What caught his attention this time and made him stop for a second look, was that the lucky Crow held a bit of cheese in her beak.

"No need to search any farther," thought the sly fox. "Here is a dainty bite for my breakfast."

Up he trotted to the foot of the tree in which the crow was sitting, and looking up admiringly, he cried, "Good-morning, beautiful creature!"

The crow, her head cocked on one side, watched the fox suspiciously. But she kept her beak tightly closed on the cheese and did not return his greeting.

"What a charming creature she is!" said the fox. "How her feathers shine! What a beautiful form and what splendid wings! Such a wonderful bird should have a very lovely voice, since everything else about her is so perfect. Could she sing just one song, I know I should hail her Queen of Birds."

Listening to these flattering words, the crow forgot all her suspicion, and also her breakfast. She wanted very much to be called Queen of birds.

So she opened her beak wide to utter her loudest caw, and down fell the cheese straight into the fox's open mouth.

"Thank you," said the fox sweetly, as he walked off. "Though it is cracked, you have a voice sure enough. But where are your wits?"

Moral : Do not get carried away by false praise.

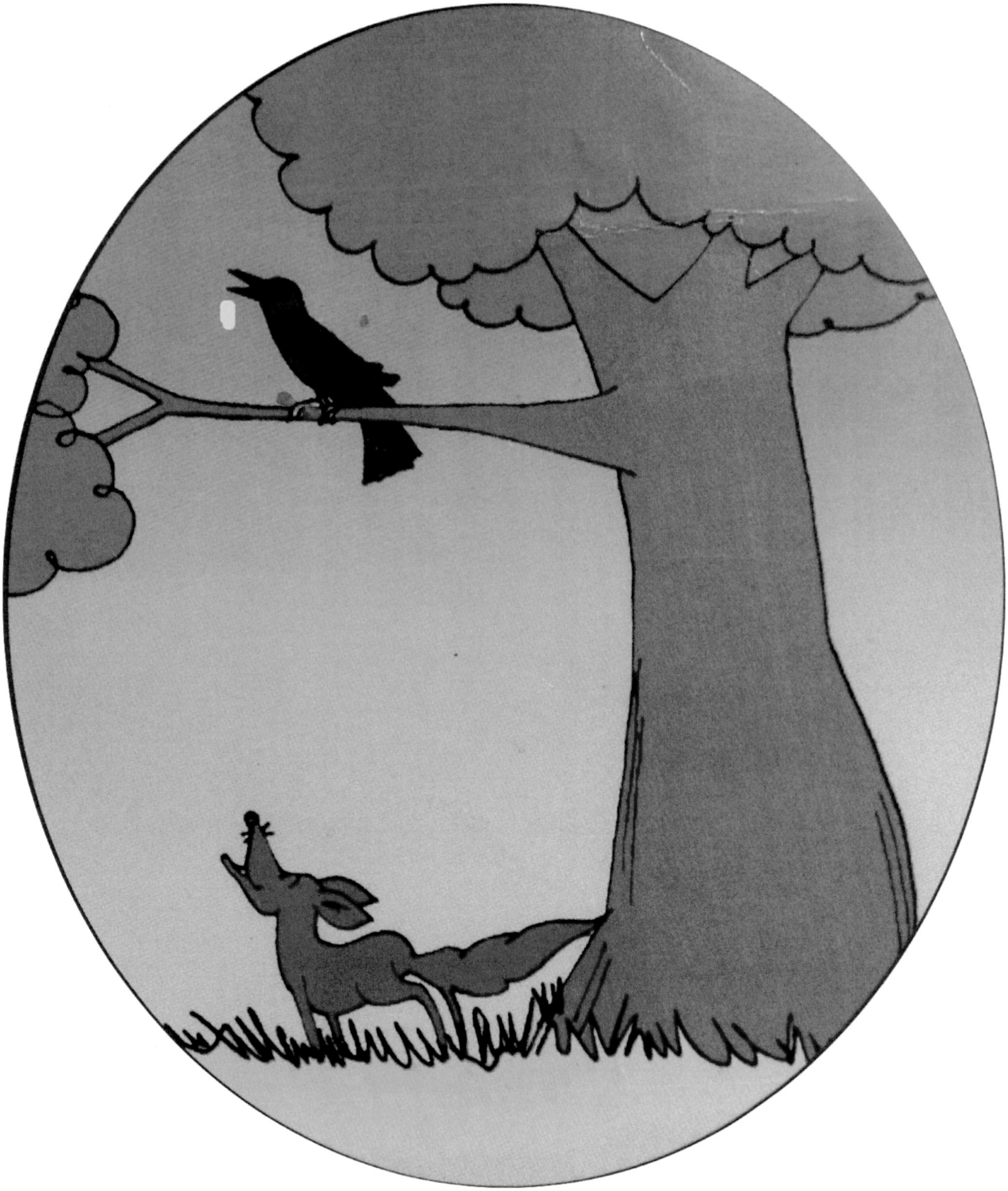

30. The Hen, the Dog and the Fox

Once a hen and a dog were close friends. They used to roam around the village. Once when they were out , it got dark early and they decided to seek shelter. They found a big tree with a hollow ints bark. The dog decided to sleep in the hollow and the hen went up the tree.

After some time, a fox saw the hen but he could not reach her. He devised a plan. "Oh dear hen! I have heard that you are a great singer. It will be my privilege to shake my hands with you and congratulate you. Could you please come down."

But the clever hen saw through his plan and said, "O Fox, Thank you for your kind words. But my singing is nothing without my musician who is sleeping in the hollow. Why don't you congratulate him first?"

The fox was delighted and he thought that probably there was another another animal in the hollow that he could eat. Thinking so, he peeped inside the hollow to catch it. But the dog, who had heard the hen, got the cue and bit the fox hard on his nose. The fox screamed in pain and ran away.

Moral : One can overcome difficult situations with wits and intelligence.

31. The Wolf and the Fox

There was a proud wolf in a forest. He used to feel that there was no one who was stronger than him. There was also a fox there. The fox said," Dear wolf, don't be proud . A man is stronger than you."

But the Wolf said, "Show me a man and I will show my power."

At that time an old man was passing that way."Yeah ! there goes a man. I will go and fight with him,"said the wolf.

"Stop! Stop! He is an old man. Let us wait for a young man," said the fox.

Meanwhile a young man came by that way. "Look! this is the man whom you have to fight with".

Immediately the wolf jumped onto the man. That man was a hunter. He had a stick in his hand.

He waited for the right moment and killed the wolf with the stick.

The fox then said to the wolf-"Now tell me whether what I said was true or false?" and left the place.

Moral : Don't act foolish based on a false pride.

32. Frog and the Cuckoo

A frog was once so impressed with the cuckoo's sweet voice that he begged the bird to teach him to sing.
"My only ambition in life is to be able to sing like you, please teach me" requested the frog.
The cuckoo agreed to take on the frog as his student. Day after day, he taught the frog.

A week passed and then two. The cuckoo tried hard but the frog could only croak in different notes. Then one day the cuckoo asked the frog that he no longer can continue the lessons. When the frog demanded to know the reason the cuckoo said, "Even after trying so hard you have not improved a bit but I fear I have learnt your habits and I have begun to croak like you. Before I lose my sweet voice and croak like you, I am stopping my lessons and will leave from here."

Moral : Certain things in nature can not be changed.

33. The Problem of the Mice

Once, a great number of mice used to live in a grocer's shop. They ate the fresh, tasty wheat, rice, bread, cheese and biscuits that were kept in the shop. They were having a great time.

But finally, concerned with the losses the baker got a cat who began chasing and killing the mice. The mice could not reach the food anymore. This was a great cause of worry for them. They decided to call a meeting of all the mice in the shop to discuss this problem.

They got together and started thinking. One of them suggested that they must get rid of the fat cat but no one could think of a way of doing so. So they kept thinking of other ways. Finally, one mouse spoke up, "We should tie anklet's on the cat's feet. That way, whenever the cat is near or is coming in our direction, we would get to know by the ringing of the anklets and we can quickly run back to our holes."

All the mice liked the suggestion and they started dancing and celebrating with joy. But their celebrations did not last very long for soon an old and experienced mouse said, "You fools! Stop celebrating and first tell me: who will tie the anklets?"

None of the mice had an answer to this question..

Moral : One should not make impossible plans.

34. The Greedy Dog

Once, a dog stole a big piece of meat from the butcher's shop. He was extremely proud of his own courage, and ran off with it, holding the meat tightly in his jaws. He wanted to quickly find a safe place to enjoy it alone at ease.

Soon the dog came to a small stream that had a plank bridge over it. The dog was crossing the plank bridge with the piece of meat in his mouth, when he happened to see his own reflection in the water. He could not understand that it was his own shadow. instead, he thought it was another dog with a meaty bone in his mouth.

Greedy as he was, the dog decided to snatch the meaty bone from the other dog. So, he flew at his reflection to snatch its bone. But alas, he dropped his own bone in the water.

Moral : Greed never pays.

35. The Monkey and the Log

Once some monkeys were sitting on a tree. The tree was at such a place, where construction of a temple was going on.

A carpenter was sawing a huge log to cut it into two parts. Just then the bell rang for the lunch break. The carpenter pushed a wedge into the split portion of the half sawed log and went to have his lunch, along with other workers. When the monkeys saw that there was nobody around, they jumped down from the tree and came near the temple. They began to play with the tools lying there. One of the monkeys, who was very curious about all those things, went round the half sawed log. Then he sat on top of it. He spread his legs on both sides of the log, whereas his tail dangled through the split portion.

Now the monkey started prying the wedge out of the log with his hands. Suddenly, the wedge came out. The split parts of the log firmly snapped shut together crushing the monkeys tail in between. The monkey cried in pain and jumped off the log, but his tail was cut off for ever.

Moral : Think before you act.

36. The Intelligent Ducks

A fox searching for its food saw a flock of ducks. It went towards them. The ducks got scared. The fox asked them - "Tell me your last wish before I kill you ! "

"Before we die we want to pray to God", the ducks said.

"Ok! Go ahead! Pray", the fox said.

One duck starred saying "Bec..Bec..."

Then, the second one started doing the same. This way one after the other all the ducks started shouting simultaneously.

The noise had a jarring effect on the fox. Unable to bear it, the fox left the ducks.

Moral : One can always get out of a danger with a good idea.

37. The Goose that laid the Golden Egg

Once upon a time there lived a farmer called Badri. He was so poor that he never had enough to eat. He visited several temples, offering his prayers to God to help him out of poverty, but they were of no avail.

Meanwhile, a holy saint, well known for his magical powers, happened to visit the village. All the villagers along with Badri queued up to meet him. He patiently waited for his turn and narrated him all his difficulties. Moved by his sad state, the holy saint created a goose and gave it to him.

"Dear Badri! This is an extraordinary goose, which lays a golden egg everyday. Please take this home and live happily with the money you get by selling the egg."

Badri was elated and praised his luck for having been blessed by the saint. Since then, he had no troubles and he also accumulated enough riches to lead a comfortable life. People who knew his story could not help turning green with jealousy.

As days passed by, one day a neighbor visited him and said,"Brother, there must be several golden eggs in this goose's stomach. If you can remove them all at once, you can build a big house with that money". Influenced by his words, Badri thought,"Just imagine! Only if I could take away all the golden eggs at once, instead of waiting for one a day, how rich would I be?"

So he got a knife and cut open the stomach of the goose, which writhed in pain and died. Hoping to find several golden eggs, when he looked inside, he was aghast to find nothing. The goose was as normal as any other goose. With his precious goose dead, Badri repented his hasty deed and cursed himself for his greed.

Moral : Too much greed will lead to a disaster.

38. The Dog and the Donkey

Once upon a time, there lived a rich man in a village. He had kept a donkey and a dog to serve as his pets. The dog used to guard his master's house and escort him wherever he went. The donkey used to carry load on his back to and fro his workplace. Both of them slept in the rich man's courtyard. Thus, they were leading their life under the kind shelter of the rich man.

The man loved his dog very much. And the dog, whenever there was a danger from thieves would bark loudly and scare them away.

This made the donkey jealous of the dog's fate. He cursed his own ill-fate; 'What a bad luck I've. My master doesn't love me in spite of my putting in hard labor. Now, I must do what this dog does to please my master.'

One night thieves entered the rich man's house to rob him. The donkey warned the dog not to bark and started braying loudly to warn the rich man. The man got frightened to see his donkey's abnormal behavior. He thought that the donkey might have gone crazy. So he picked up a stick and beat up the donkey till it fell on the ground.

Meanwhile, the robbers entered the house easily and stole away all valuable articles.

Later the rich man was shocked to see his house burgled.

Moral : Jealousy is harmful.

39. The Three Fishes

Long, long ago, there lived three fishes with their families in a pond. Their names were Anagatavidhata, Pratyutpannamati and Yadbhavishya. Anagatavidhata was very practical. She always planned her actions in advance. Pratyutpannamati too was practical and always tendered good will to her elder sister Anagatavidhata. Yadbhavishya, the youngest of them all, loved to only laze around. She didn't like to work at all.

One day, some fishermen came to the pond. One of them said, "This is the pond I was telling you about. There are many fish in this pond. Let's come here tomorrow and catch all of them."

Anagatavidhata overheard the fishermen's talk. She gathered all the fish in the pond and narrated to them what she had heard about. She said, "It's better that we move out of here to some other safer pond. Our life will, at least, be safe." Everybody agreed to this proposal including Pratyutpannamati.

But Yadbhavishya said, "I don't think the fishermen will really come tomorrow. We need not be afraid and run away like cowards."

But Anagatavidhata and Pratyutpannamati didn't agree with Yadbhavishya's ideas. The next morning, the fishermen came to the pond. They cast their net in the pond. Anagatavidhata had already moved out to another pond early in the morning. Pratyutpannamati was unable to move out when the fishermen came, so she pretended to be dead. However Yadbhavishya continued to sleep without any concern.

The fishermen discarded Pratyutpannamati thinking her to be dead and trapped Yadbhavishya and took her with them.

Moral : Always plan for your future intelligently.

40. The Young Rabbit

A rabbit family lived happily in a burrow outside a rich man's garden. There were four children in the family and the youngest rabbit was very naughty. He never listened to any good advise. The father and mother rabbit's were protective of their children and never let them out of their sight.

One day the four young rabbits decided to explore the outside world. The mother rabbit warned them not to go inside the garden. She told them that the gardner was a mean guy and could hurt them. The four rabbits promised their mother that they will be careful.

However the youngest rabbit was curious and he secretly stepped aside and sneaked into the garden. The garden was beautiful and there were lot of fruits. The youngest rabbit got tempted and went near the fruits. There were four guard dogs who immediately came and started chasing him. The gardner heard the ruckus and saw the rabbit. He took a stick and he too, started to chase the rabbit.

With great difficulty the young rabbit was able to save himself and he went home. He decided that he will always listen to his parents in future.

Moral: Always listen to good advise of elders.

41. Troubles from the Relatives

In a big desert there was some fertile land and oasis also. A camel used to stay near the oasis. Grass was plenty around the oasis.

Once the camel fell sick. It was unable to get up. The camel's relatives and friends started to come over to pay a visit making long journeys to reach that place. Being tired they all rested over the grass. The oasis got dried up.

After a few days the camel regained its health. It searched for grass as it was hungry. There was no grass anywhere near. The camel went out in search of another oasis.

Moral : One must be careful with those who consume all your stuff

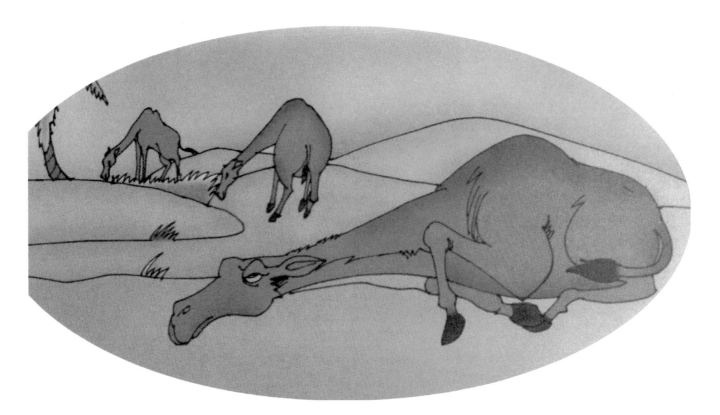

42. The Fox and the Cat

A cat and a fox were once discussing about hounds.

The cat said, "I hate hounds. They are very nasty animals. They hunt and kill us."

The fox said, "I hate hounds more than you".

The cat asked, "How do you save yourself from hounds?"

The fox replied, "There are many tricks to get away from hounds."

The cat asked." Can you say what your tricks are?"

"They are very simple", said the fox. He added, "I can hide behind thick bushes. I can run along thorny hedges. I can hide in burrows. There are many more such tricks".

Now it was the turn of the fox to ask the cat about her tricks.

The fox asked, "How many tricks do you know?"

The cat replied, "I know just one trick."

The fox sneered, "Oh! How sad! You know only one trick? What is your trick ?"

The cat was about to answer. But, she found a flock of hounds fast approach.

She said,"I am going to do it now, because, the hounds are coming".

Saying these words, the cat ran up a nearby tree safe from the hounds. The fox tried all his tricks but the hounds caught him.

"My one trick is better than all his tricks", said the cat to herself.

Moral : It is better to be a master of one art than to be a jack of many arts.

43. The Frogs who Rode the Snake

There lived a brown snake by the name of Mandvishya near a pond. The pond was full of frogs - big and small. They were all leading a happy life under the good rule of their king frog. The big brown snake had become old and weak and could no more catch his prey easily for his meals. So he decided to play a ruse upon the frogs. One day, he went to the pond and lay there as if he was suffering from illness. After sometime, the king frog happened to come out of water. He saw the brown snake lying by the side of the pond in a pitiable condition. When he asked for the reason in a frightened tone, the snake said, "A week before, I bit the son of a pundit by mistake, because he had tried to kill me with a stick. He died immediately. Now the pundit has cursed me. According to his curse, I'll have to serve the frogs and have to eat whatever they offer me for food. So, I'm here to serve you."

The king frog and his ministers were delighted to hear this. Other frogs also gathered around the snake. Many of the minister frogs and the king frog too jumped on to the back of the brown snake to have a joy ride. The brown snake swam around the pond with all the frogs riding on his back.

The next day also the frogs rode over the entire length of the snake's back. The snake swam in the pond. Soon the king frog realized that the snake's movement had slowed down. When he asked for the reason, the brown snake said, "Your Majesty, due to constant swimming and non-availability of food, I've gone weak. I can't move any more now."

The king frog, thinking that in view of the snake's physical weakness, he might not be able to have joy rides in future, allowed the snake to eat a few frogs.

The brown snake, thus, started eating the frogs easily, one by one. One day, there were no frogs left in the pond, except the king frog. So the snake spoke to the king frog. "I can't remain hungry anymore. There are no frogs now left in the pond except you. So, please excuse me for eating you." And the brown snake attacked the frog with a lightening speed and ate him.

Moral : Never trust your enemy.

44. The Revenge of the Crow

Once upon a time, there stood a huge tree on the outskirts of a small village. On this tree, there lived a pair of crows with their young ones. And at the root of the tree there lived a big serpent in a deep hole. Every time the crows laid their eggs, the serpent crept up the tree and ate all the eggs and the young ones. With the result, the crows were never able to raise their young ones. This made the crows very sad. They didn't know how to get rid of the killer serpent.

One day, the crows went to a fox. The fox was their good friend.

"Hello dear friends, come in", said the fox seeing the crows at her door, "You two seem to be very sad. What's the matter?"

"The root cause of our problem is a bad serpent. He is after us. He eats up our eggs and the young ones. Please help us get rid of this serpent," said the female crow to the fox.

The fox too was shocked to hear this sad story. She promised to help the crows. She thought for a few minutes and then laid out a plan before the crows.

"Listen carefully", said the fox, "you know where the king's palace is situated. You've also seen the queen taking bath in an open swimming pool, inside the palace. The queen, while taking bath always removes all her ornaments and keeps them on a tray kept by the side of the pool. While she is busy taking her bath, you two swoop down upon the tray and pick up a gold necklace from it. Drop them into the serpent's hole. The servants of the queen will come chasing you and finding the necklace in the serpent's hole, they will first kill the serpent to save them from being bitten by it and then will take the necklace out of the hole. Thus, the serpent will be killed and you too will be saved from all the troubles of killing it yourself."

This was a very bright idea. The crows liked it. They flew to the king's palace. There they saw the queen taking bath in a swimming pool. She had removed her ornaments and kept them in a tray.

The crows swooped down upon the tray, picked up one expensive diamond necklace from it and flew towards the snake's hole. The guards ran after the crows brandishing their sticks and swords.

They chased the crows and soon reached that big tree, where the big snake lived. They found the diamond necklace, lying inside the serpent's hole. Afraid of the snake, they first killed the snake with sticks and swords and then took out the ornament and returned to the palace.

The crows thanked the fox for her help and lived happily in the tree, thereafter.

Moral : Intelligence is greater than physical strength.

45. The Ant and the Goddess

Once an ant lived near a temple. One day the ant was very hungry and after searching for a long time, found a loaf of bread. Just when it was about to eat the bread, a stray dog came and ran away with the bread.

The ant continued its search and soon found some grains of rice. Just when the ant reached the place, a strong gush of wind blew away the grains.

Not giving up, the ant went further and found some sugar. But alas! suddenly it began to rain heavily and washed away the sugar. With nowhere else to go, the ant went to the temple and prayed to the Goddess.

The Goddess was moved with pity and she appeared before the ant. She gave the ant all the things back that were taken away from her. The grateful ant thanked the Goddess.

Moral : God helps those who first try to help themselves.

46. The Tiger and the Goat

One day, a goat was grazing on a patch of green grass when suddenly he heard a sound. Quickly turning round, he found that an old tiger was following him. It was too late for him to run; so he stood his ground and faced the tiger, ready to meet any attack.

The tiger, turning to the goat, said, "I see you are ready to fight, but why should we both get hurt fighting? If you can tell me any three truths, I shall let you go away."

"All right," said the goat, "I shall tell you three simple truths about yourself and me. The first truth is this: if you go and tell the other tigers that you met me here and still you didn't kill me, they will not believe you."

"Too true," said the tiger, "Go on, tell me the other two."

"Well", said the goat, "suppose I get away and tell the other goats that you did not want to fight, they will not believe me."

"Too true", said the tiger, "go on, tell me the next truth."

"The next truth is this," said the goat, "we are both talking here and you are listening to all I say without trying to kill me. So you cannot be really hungry."

"Yes, yes," said the tiger, "go in peace, you clever fellow, remember but the next time we meet, there will be no more talking. You will not live to open your mouth again."

"Ah!" said the goat, "there is yet one more truth, the last. It is that you will never catch me another time." So saying, the goat ran away and took good care that the tiger never caught him again.

Moral : Wits are more important than physical strength.

47. Help! Help!!

Once there was a farmer named Rama who lived in a village near the forest. He had a son name Raju. Everyday the father used to take his sheep and buffaloes to the forest for grazing.

One day he took his son, Raju, also along with him. Raju was a very mischievous boy and always played pranks. He was also a habitual liar. Rama tried to correct his son but it was all in vain.

They soon found a good spot for the cattle to graze. Rama asked his son to watch the cattle and went to take a nap under a big tree.

While he was resting, suddenly he heard Raju yelling, " Help! Help! Lion, Lion! Father come fast. Help me".

Rama got up quickly and ran towards Raju. But as soon as he reached there, he saw that Raju was laughing at his prank. The annoyed father went back to his sleep.

After some more time, again he heard Raju screaming,"Help! Help! Tiger, Tiger! Help me father!"

Rama again got up and rushed to the spot only to see that he was fooled again. He yelled at his son and warned him not to play the prank again.

After some time, a real tiger came to the spot. Raju trembled with fear and manage to shout again, "Help! Help! Tiger, Tiger! Father come fast !"

Rama heard his screams but thought that the boy was again playing a prank and ignored him. He peacefully went back to his sleep.

The tiger attacked Raju and killed him. Raju had to pay a heavy price for his mischief.

Moral : No one believes a habitual liar.

48. A Costly Help

Once upon a time, a wild poisonous snake lived in a forest. The cobra was evil and used to bite any animal that it came across. Hence fearing for their live, all animals were careful and stayed away from him.

One day the snake went out to hunt for its prey. While he was searching for food, suddenly the bushes caught fire and the snake was trapped in it. There was no way out and the cobra started crying, "Help ! Help!"

None of the animals came to his rescue. There was a man who was traveling through the forest and he heard the cries of the snake. Out of pity he decided to rescue the snake.

He took a wooden stick from the branch of a tree and pulled out the snake with it.

But the moment the snake came out, he went back to his old evil and selfish behavior. Instead of thanking the man for saving its life, he went ahead and bit the man.

The man learnt his lesson that he should not help a bad person. If we help evil people it will only cause harm to us.

Moral : Do not help a wicked person.

49. The King of Frogs

There lived some frogs in a pond. They were happy and content with their life. One day they decided to get a new king and prayed to God. God heard their prayers and sent a wooden log as their new king. For some time the frogs liked their new king but later they found him to be unresponsive and hence changed their minds. They again prayed to God and requested for a new king.

This time God sent a stork as their new king. The frogs were happy with their new king. But soon they realized that the stork was eating one frog daily and their numbers were reducing.

They repented and prayed to God to take back the king and decided to stay without a king as before.

Moral : Be content with what you have.

50. The Monkey and the Crocodile

Long, long ago, there lived a huge crocodile in the river Ganges. The river flew through a dense jungle. On both sides of the river there stood tall berry and other fruit trees. On one such tree there lived a big monkey by the name of Raktamukha. He ate fruits from the tree and passed his days happily jumping from one tree to another. Sometimes, he climbed down the tree; took a bath in the river and rested for a while on its bank.

One day, the crocodile came out of the river and sat under the big berry tree in which the monkey lived. The monkey who was sitting high on a branch saw the crocodile taking rest under the tree. He became very eager to talk to the crocodile and cultivate a friendship with him.

"Since you're taking rest under the tree", said the monkey, "you're my guest. It's my duty to offer you food."

The monkey gave berries and other fruits to the crocodile to eat. The crocodile ate them and thanked the monkey for his hospitality. The monkey and the crocodile talked together for hours and soon they became friends. They developed such friendship that neither of the two was happy to miss each other's company even for a single day. Early since morning, the monkey would start looking for the crocodile, and the crocodile would also swim up to the berry tree as early as possible. They would sit together, have a hearty chat and the monkey would offer him the delicious berries. This became their daily routine.

One day, the monkey gave some fruits to the crocodile for his wife, as well. The crocodile took the fruits happily to his wife and also narrated the whole story to her.

The next day, the crocodile's wife said to her husband, "Dear, if these fruits are so tasty, then the monkey who eats these fruits must be ten times more tasty. Why don't you bring the heart of this monkey for my meals?"

The crocodile was shocked to hear these words from his wife. He said, "Dear, the monkey is my friend. It would not be fair to take his heart away from him."

"That means, you don't love me", said the crocodile's wife and began to cry.

"Don't cry, dear", said the crocodile. "I'll bring the monkey's heart for you."

The crocodile swiftly swam to the other bank of the river and reached the tree where the monkey lived.

"My wife and I invite you to our home for a dinner. My wife is very angry with me for not having invited you earlier," the crocodile said in a sad tone.

"But how will I go with you?" asked the monkey. "I don't know how to swim."

"Don't worry", said the crocodile. "Just ride on my back. I'll take you to my house."

The monkey happily sat on the back of the crocodile and the crocodile started his journey in the water.

While in mid stream, the monkey became frightened to see the water all around him and asked the crocodile to swim at a slow speed so that he did not fall into the river.

The crocodile thought that he could reveal his real intentions to the monkey, since it was impossible for him to escape from the middle of the river. So he said to the monkey, "I am taking you to my home to please my wife. She wants to eat your heart. She says that since you eat tasty fruits day and night, your heart must be ten times more tasty than those fruits."

The monkey was taken aback to hear these words. He had never expected this from a friend. He kept his mental cool and said wittingly, "Very well friend. It would be my privilege to offer my heart to your charming wife. But alas! You didn't inform me earlier, otherwise, I'd have carried my heart with me. Which I usually keep in the hollow of the tree."

"Oh!" said the crocodile, "I didn't think of it earlier. Now we'll have to go back to the tree."

The crocodile turned and swam back to the bank of the river where the monkey lived.

Upon reaching the bank the monkey jumped off the crocodile's back and quickly climbed up his home tree. The crocodile waited for hours together for the monkey to return carrying his heart.

When the crocodile realized that the monkey was taking too long searching for his heart, he called him from the ground and said, "Friend, I believe, you must have found your heart by now. Now, please come down. My wife must be waiting for us and getting worried."

But the monkey laughed and said sitting at the top of the tree, "My dear foolish friend. You've deceived me as a friend. Can any one take out his heart and keep that in a hollow? It was all a trick to save my life and teach a lesson to a treacherous friend like you. Now get lost."

The crocodile returned home empty handed.

Moral : At times, presence of mind pays well.

51. The Hare and the Tortoise

Once a hare and a tortoise were good friends. One day the hare invited the tortoise to his home for dinner. However the hare wanted to play a prank so when the tortoise reached there, the hare said, "I waited for you for a long time. But as you walk slow, you took too long to come here. Sorry the dinner is over."

The angry tortoise knew that the hare was playing a prank, but he kept quiet. Next day the tortoise invited the hare for dinner. The hare did not wanted to give an opportunity to the tortoise to take revenge, so he reached very early to the tortoise's house. The tortoise welcomed him and said,"Dear friend, the dinner is ready. Why don't you wash your hands and feet before you eat. Please wipe your feet on the mat near the door when you return."

The hare ran out to the water stream outside and washed his feet and hands. He wiped his feet on the mat. But as he came towards the dinner table, the tortoise yelled, "Stop Friend! look your feet are so dirty. They are leaving black marks every where, please wash them properly."

Again the hare ran to wash his feet and then wiped them on the mat. But again the tortoise stopped him. This happened many times.

The tortoise had crushed black coal and kept it on the mat. So each time, the rabbit wiped his feet on the mat, the coal stuck to his feet and made the black marks. Finally the hare gave up and ran away to his home.

Moral : Tit for tat.

52. Who is Oldest?

Once an elephant and a monkey were good friends. They would always boast and tell fancy tales about themselves whenever they met. Each one wanted to outdo the other.

One day they sat under a big old tree near the river. The tree was said to be over 100 years old. The monkey said, " I am the oldest animal in this forrest. I was born when this tree had its first flower blossom."

"No my dear friend, I am older than you. Because I was born when this tree was just a sapling."

They continued their argument. The crow, on the top of the tree, heard them fighting. He said, "Stop your silly fight. I was the one who planted this tree. So I am older than both of you", and flew away.

Moral : Don't fight over silly matter.

53. The Greedy Fox

Once upon a time, in a dense forest there lived a fox. One day, as usual, the fox went out for hunting but could not hunt even a single animal. He roamed in the forest the entire day in search of food and finally found a piece of meat near the river. Just when he was about to eat the meat, he saw the carcass of a deer on the other side of the river.

Tempted, the fox took the meat in his mouth and ran towards the deer. But in his hurry, he dropped the piece of meat in the water.

He consoled himself saying that he can still feast on the deer. He reached the other side and got the deer. He thought to take the deer to his home on the other side of the river and relish on it for the next few days.

As he pulled the deer along with him, he fell down into the river along with the carcass. A crocodile in the river caught up and feasted on both the fox as well as the deer.

Moral : Greed is harmful.

54. The Two Ploughs

There was a blacksmith in a small town. He used to make different tools and sell it in his shop. One day he made two ploughs. He thought that he can sell them to some farmers and get good amount in return. The two ploughs were extremely different in their natures. One of them was very eager to help a farmer and was ready to work hard. The other plough was lazy and wanted to just sit idle without doing any work.

The next day a farmer came and purchased the plough who worked hard. The plough helped the farmer a lot and the farmer became rich in due time.

After an year, he took the plough to the blacksmith and decided to get one more plough to help him. He wanted to buy a similar plough.

The farmers plough saw his old friend, the lazy one, sitting in a corner and rusting. He asked, "Brother, are you not happy here? I see that you are rusted?"

The lazy plough was surprised to see the farmers plough glowing with no signs of rust. He asked, "Brother I do not work and yet I have rusted so much. How are you maintaining your beauty? Please tell me the secret."

The farmers plough laughed and said, "I work hard and help the farmer. He takes great care to maintain me. He oils me every day and that is the only secret that I still look so young."

The lazy plough immediately understood the importance of hard work and decided to mend his ways.

Moral : Hard work always pays.

101 Panchatantra Tales							86							Vyanst

55. The Faithful Mongoose

Once upon a time, there lived a poor Brahmin with his wife in a small village. The Brahmin used to perform puja at religious functions taking place in nearby villages. They had no children. They offered prayers to God for a child. At last, a son was born to them.

The Brahmin's wife had a mongoose as her pet. The mongoose was very playful. It used to guard the Brahmin's house and also protect the baby, when he slept in the cradle.

Once, some people came to invite the Brahmin for performing puja at their house. The Brahmin was in a dilemma. Should he go to perform puja or stay home to look after his baby? His wife had also gone to fetch water from the well situated on the outskirts of the village.

The Brahmin didn't want to leave the baby all alone in the house, even though the mongoose was sitting there beside the cradle like a baby sitter. He was in a state of dilemma.

But at last he buckled under the pressure and went to the nearby village to conduct the religious ceremony, leaving the baby all alone in the house with the mongoose.

The mongoose still sat beside the cradle guarding the baby. Suddenly, he saw a big snake crawling towards the cradle. Being a natural enemy of snakes and also having the responsibility of guarding the baby, he pounced upon the snake. After a fierce fighting with the snake, the mongoose killed it.

But the mouth and paws of the mongoose were smeared with the snake's blood. The mongoose was happy that he had done his duty faithfully and had saved the baby from the snake. He ran to the main entrance of the house and sat there waiting for his master's wife to come bzack. He thought that she would be highly impressed with his performance and shall reward him suitably.

After sometime, the Brahmin's wife came along with the water pitcher on her head. She saw the paws and mouth of the mongoose smeared in blood. She thought that the mongoose had killed her baby. In a fit of rage, she threw the heavy water pitcher on the head of the mongoose. The mongoose died on the spot.

The Brahmin's wife now went running inside the house. There she saw a big snake lying dead. The baby was sleeping safe in the cradle. Now she realized that she was greatly mistaken, and the mongoose had, in fact, saved her child. She began repenting and weeping. She had killed her faithful pet without knowing what had really happened.

Moral : Haste makes waste

56. The Monkeys and the Bird

Long, long ago, there lived a troop of monkeys in a hilly region. When winter fell, the monkeys began to shiver with cold. They had no place to protect themselves. One of the monkeys suggested that they should go to the nearby village and take shelter in the houses of human beings till the winter lasted. His suggestion was accepted by all the monkeys. All of them shifted from the hilly region to an adjoining village.

But, next morning, when the villagers saw a big troop of monkeys, all of a sudden, jumping from branches to branches and on their rooftops, they greeted them by pelting stones and showing sticks. Thus, the monkeys, instead of getting shelter in the village, were compelled to retreat to the hilly region and face the chilly winds and the snowfalls once again.

Then, ultimately one of the monkeys thought of making a fire to warm up the surrounding. He had seen the villagers sitting around fire and warming up themselves. There were some red berry trees around. The monkeys mistook them for burning coals.

They plucked those berries and placed them under a pile of dry sticks. They tried to make a fire by blowing into the pile. They huffed and puffed, but alas! there was no fire. The monkeys became sad.

There were also a few birds who lived in the same tree where the monkeys lived. Seeing the plight of the monkeys, one of the birds said to them, "What a fool you are, trying to make fire from those red fruits. Have the fruits ever made fire? Why don't all of you take shelter in the nearby cave?"

When the monkeys saw the birds advising them they became red with rage. One old monkey said, "You dare call us fools. Why do you poke your nose into our affairs?"

But the little bird kept on chirping and advising the monkeys. Then one huge monkey caught hold of the neck of the noisy bird and dashed it against the tree trunk. The bird died on the spot.

Moral : Do not advise an idiot.

57. The Fox and the Goats

One day three goats were grazing in a forest on one side of a river. It was getting dark and they decided to return back to their home on the other side of the river. There was a narrow wooden plank set as a bridge and they to started to cross the river on it.

Suddenly they saw a fox, on the opposite side, coming towards them. There was no way to escape and the goats panicked thinking that the fox will surely kill them.

However the older goat told them that they need to stick together and devised a plan. They lined up themselves such that the strongest goat was in the front and the weakest one was at the back. As soon as the fox got near to them, they pushed him together with all their strength. The fox was not prepared for this sudden attack and he lost his balance. The fox fell into the river and was drowned. The three clever goats saved themselves by working together.

Moral : Unity is the real strength.

58. The Dog with the Little Bell

Once a farmer had a dog which had the bad habit of biting anyone who came within its reach. He scared away many guests and was a source of embarrassment for his master.

For this reason, its master hung a little bell on the collar around its neck, so that everybody would be warned of the dog's approach and could take care not to get too close to its fearsome teeth and extremely powerful jaws.

The dog was very proud of its little bell and liked to boast that the tinkle of it scared men away.

A wise old dog on the farm, however, warned it:

" The bell resounds to your shame not to your glory".

Moral : One should not be proud of a shameful act.

59. The Rooster and the Fox

Once a fox was wandering near a village. He saw a beautiful rooster sitting on the top of a tree at a considerable height. 'How can I have this rooster for my meal,' thought the fox to himself. He knew, he could not climb up the tree to kill the rooster.

Applying his cleverness, the fox said to the rooster, "How is it that you are sitting higher up on the tree? Don't you know that it has been decided in a meeting of animals today that from now an animals and birds will not kill each other for food. Bigger fish will not eat smaller fish."

"That means the king lion, tigers and leopards shall start eating grass from today," said the rooster, outwitting the fox.

But, the fox wasn't ready to give up so easily. "This point needs clarification," said the fox cunningly. "Come down, we'll go together to our king and request him to clarify this point."

"We needn't go there," said the rooster. "I can see some of your friends coming towards us"

"Who are they?" the fox asked in surprise.

"Hounds," the rooster replied.

"Hounds!" the fox repeated the words in fear and sprang up on his feet to run away.

"Why do you run away? You have just told that all the animals and birds have became friends to each other," the rooster said laughing.

"But, perhaps the hounds might not have heard of this meeting," the fox replied and ran away into the deep forest.

Moral : Do not believe your enemy.

60. The Ant and the Elephant

One day, an elephant was enjoying itself by playing in the lake and walking and running all about. It came upon an anthill.

The ants were so horrified of the elephant that they said in unison "Dear elephant, leave us alone and please do not kill us."

Hearing this, the elephant shouted with pride, "I am going to kill you all and won't spare any of you."

The elephant stepped forward to kill the ants, but the ants smartly climbed onto him. Some of them started biting his legs. Some of the ants bit his trunk, some of them bit his ears and two of them got into his eyes. The elephant shouted in pain, but the ants kept biting.

The pain was so intense that the elephant ran in all directions and accidentally fell into a deep creek and died. That was the end of the cruel elephant and the ants lived peacefully.

Moral : One should not be proud of a shameful act.

61. The Lion and the Mouse

Once, a lion, the king of the animals, caught a mouse.

"Ah! I was resting quietly but you have disturbed me. I will kill you" the lion roared.

The mouse was scared for his life.

"Oh, The king! Please leave me. I will remember you for ever. Whenever it is necessary I shall return the favor" begged the mouse.

"You are a small animal ! How will you do a favor to me ? What can you do ? You are just a tiny creature ", the lion laughed and said.

But the lion was amused and decided to forgive the mouse. The mouse thanked and went away.

Few days passed. Once a hunter threw his net and caught the lion in the trap. He tied the net with thick ropes. The lion roared loudly. The hunter went to town to bring a cart to carry the lion. The lion tried his best to escape. But all his attempts bear no fruits. At that moment the small mouse came there. The mouse saw the lion in distress. Immediately the mouse with its strong teeth cut the rope and the net.

The lion was amazed to see a tiny animal doing such a great job. He realized that the mouse was the same mouse which he had not killed earlier.

"Good! Oh mouse! Though you are a tiny animal you can do a powerful job. You have returned the favor to me as said earlier. I thank you", the lion said.

The mouse was happy that he helped the lion.

Moral : Even a powerless person can help others.

62. The Chicken and the Cat

Once upon a time, there lived some hens and a cat on a poultry farm. The hens were scared of the cat, since, she was known to eat hens and chickens. The little chickens were warned not to leave the coop and wander around.

One day, one of the little chick went astray and left her friends. The cat saw the little chicken and was tempted. The cat thought to herself, 'I can easily catch the chicken and eat her for lunch.'

However the chicken was still far and the cat was unable to cross the boundary. The cat said, "How are you my, dear friend? Why don't you come near and I will show you a great place where you can get more food? "

The little chick was scared that the cat was trying to get close to her by asking her well-being. Fearing her death, the chick said to the cat, "Thank you for your concern. My mother had warned me of strangers and you are the only thing I fear. Please stay away from me". Saying so the little chicken rushed away to be back with her friends.

Moral : Beware of strangers.

63. The Tortoise and the Sun God

Once upon a time, the Sun God hosted a grand feast to which he invited all the animals. Everyone got there punctually, except the tortoise, who never wanted to get out of his beloved home. The Sun God was furious. He went to the tortoise and shouted, "Where have you been? Why did you not come to the feast?"

Replied the tortoise, "I love my home and proud of it. I cannot leave it even for a moment and just didn't feel like going out."

"In that case," replied the angry Sun God, "Why don't you always carry your home with you!"

As soon as he had said that, the animal found a heavy shell on his back. And, ever since, the tortoise has carried his home on his back.

Moral : False pride is dangerous.

64. The Crows and the Sparrow

Once upon a time, there was a very big forest. There on a huge banyan tree lived many crows. They were selfish and arrogant. They had no friends, as no one liked them.

One day a small sparrow was returning to her nest. When she was passing by the banyan tree, it started raining. "I will stay here for a while until it stops raining," thought the little sparrow, " And I take rest on the banyan tree for a while."

The selfish crows saw her perching on the tree. One of them shouted, "Get off the tree. This tree belongs to us. Or we will peck you."

All the sparrow's pleas fell on deaf ears and she found no other way except to fly off. She went to a nearby tree, where luckily she found a hollow in a broken branch. She took her shelter there. Shortly after, the rain became heavy followed by thunderstorm.Many of the branches of the tree in which the crows had taken shelter were damaged and hurt by the wind. But the sparrow was safe inside the hollow place on her tree.

One of the crows said, "Look at the sparrow! How comfortable she is. Let us go there."

Another crow said, "I do not think she will let us share the hollow. We did not have sympathy for her when she was in need of this tree."

Then another crow said, "We should not have been so rude. We forgot that we may need help someday."

Suddenly the sparrow called out, "Come! My friends! Come to this hollow. Or you will get hurt. The rain is not going to stop soon. It seems that it may rain for a long time."

The crows flew down to the hollow and thanked the sparrow. They also apologized for their behavior.

Moral : Never be so selfish as to hurt others.

65. The King's Problem

Once there lived a king who was extremely fond of laddu's. The royal chef used to make lot of laddu's to make him happy. But the laddu's attracted lots of rats and they caused havoc in the palace. Finally the king decided to get cats to get rid of the rats. Soon there were over one hundred cats roaming the palace. They ate all the rats and everyone was happy. But now the cats started stealing food and milk from the kitchen. Soon the cats themselves became a great menace.

The king now ordered to get dogs to chase the cats away. As soon as the dogs came, the cats ran away. But the hundred dogs gave a new problem, they kept everyone awake at night with their barking. They bit any visitors to the palace and created a huge mess. So the king now ordered elephants to get rid of the dogs.

The mighty elephants drove away all the dogs. But it was difficult to maintain the elephants. The elephants were always hungry and ate lot of food leading to a huge shortage of food.

The king thought for a while and decided to get the rats back to chase the elephants away. And so the rats again came back to the palace.

Moral : An incorrect solution to a problem can lead to many more problems.

66. The Old Woman and the Tiger

An old woman lived in a small village near a forest. Her daughter was married to a rich man's son on the other side of the forest. One day the old woman decided to meet her daughter. She took a small bag carrying gifts for her daughter and son-in-law. As she was walking through the forest, suddenly a tiger stood in front of her. The tiger was hungry and delighted to see her. But the old woman was clever, she said, "O tiger! I am a poor lean old woman. You can hardly satisfy your hunger by eating me. I am visiting my daughter on the other side. She is married into a rich family. I will stay with her for a month and eat good food and get fat. Then you can eat me."

The tiger thought for a while and said, "OK, but do come back after one month else I will go to your daughter's house and eat her."

The old woman promised to return. She went to her daughter and told her the whole story. She stayed with her daughter for a month and with a heavy heart decided to go back to the forest to become the tiger's prey. But her daughter was also a very clever woman. She gave some chilly powder to the old woman and whispered a plan in her ears. She then got a round drum and made her mother sit inside it. The drum rolled and carried the old woman with it.

Soon the drum reached the tiger who was surprised to see it. He thought that the old woman was playing a trick and opened the lid. When he saw the old woman, he was angry. He said, "So you wanted to escape from me?"

But the old woman pleaded and said, "No tiger, I am ready to be your prey. But don't you want me to go to the river and wash myself?"

The tiger was happy but he did not wanted to risk the old woman escaping again. So he said, "OK fine, But I will also go along with you to the river".

Saying so, they both went too the river. The tiger also decided to take bath. The old woman quickly took out the chilly powder that her daughter gave and blew it into the tigers eyes. The tiger was caught unaware and he screamed in pain. Unable to see anything the tiger drowned himself in the river.

The old woman happily went back to her home.

Moral : You can defeat a formidable enemy with your intelligence and wits.

67. The Goat and the Clever Fox

One day a fox searching for food fell down into a deep well. He tried hard but could not get out. After some time a goat passed by and asked the fox what he was doing down there in the well.

The clever fox replied, "Did you not hear about the great drought forecast? I jumped down here to be sure to have enough water for me. Why don't you come down too?"

The goat thanked the fox for his advice and jumped into the well. But the fox immediately jumped on her back and managed to get out of the well.

The fox, once safe outside, said,

"Good bye friend! Remember never to trust the advice of a man in difficulties".

Moral : Do not trust the advise of a man in difficulties.

68. The Goat and the Elephant

Once a goat and an elephant were great friends. They always used to be together roaming around the forest. One day, while roaming, they came to the bank of a river. Near the shore there was a big tree with some strange fruits on it. The goat had a desire to eat the fruits. But she could not reach the top of the tree and she became sad. The elephant asked her about the same and then said, "Dear goat! Do not be sad, I can pluck the fruits with my trunk."

The elephant plucked the fruits, but while doing so he broke the nest of a little bird and the bird fell into the river.

The goat, who saw this, jumped into the river to save the bird. She tried hard to stay afloat but she could not swim and cried, "Help! Help!!"

The elephant was touched by the goat's act and he too jumped into the river. He placed both the goat, as well as the bird, on his back and swam safely back to the shore.

"Dear Goat! You are truly a great person. I am a stranger, but yet you risked your life to save me. Thank you very much. I can never repay your debt", said the little bird.

"Dear bird, it is basic humanity to save anyone in danger. I am not great. I am sorry for the loss of your nest, but we will help you rebuild it. Let us be friends", said the goat.

The three of them became great friends. The little bird used to bring them many strange fruits from different trees and they lived happily ever after.

Moral : An act of kindness always touches the heart.

69. The Hasty Fox

It was a windy day. Strong wind blew so hard that there was a whiz sound throughout the forest. A fox was very frightened. He ran and hide himself behind a big tree.

All of a sudden, he heard a big thud sound near him. He sprang up and ran through the forest. He started hooting "The sky has given way and fallen down."

On his way he met a deer. The deer asked, "Hey fox! Why are you running?"

The fox answered, "Didn't you hear the sound? The sky has fallen down."

The deer too started running.

They both met a zebra. On hearing the matter, the zebra also started running. As the three ran they were joined by a giraffe, a jackal, a rabbit, a wolf, a deer and many more animals.

A lion heard the noise and came out of his den. He asked, "What is the matter?"

All animals said in chorus, "The sky has fallen down."

The fox said, "I saw a portion of a sky falling down."

The lion asked, "Can you show me the place?"

The fox led all the animals to the tree. There, they found a mango lying.

The lion said, "Here is the portion of the sky which has fallen down".

Now, all the animals were ashamed of their immature behavior.

Moral : Herd instinct lead to chaos.

70. The Clever Goat

Once upon a time there was an old goat. One day, when it was getting dark, she was returning home with many other goats. She was old and weak, and when she got tired, she was left behind. It became quite dark, and as she could not find her way back, she decided to enter a cave that she saw nearby. The cave was dark and empty. It was a lion's cave who had gone out for hunting.

After some time the lion returned back to find a strange creature in his cave. All he could see were two strange glowing red eyes.The goat saw the lion and she was terribly frightened and stood still for a moment, then she thought of a plan.

"If I try to run," she thought, "the lion will soon catch me, but if I pretend not to be afraid of him I may manage to save my life." She just sat there boldly and raised her eyes. The darkness in the cave gave an impression as if it was devil itself.

"Who are you?," asked the lion.

"I am the Queen of the Goats," she replied. "I came here to eat a hundred tigers, twenty-five elephants and ten lions. I have already eaten the hundred tigers and the twenty five elephants and now I am looking for the ten lions."

The lion was very much surprised to hear this, and believing the goat had really come to devour him, he ran out of the cave saying that he was going to wash his face in the river.

As he was rushing out, he met a jackal who seeing the king of the beasts in a panic, asked what the matter was.

The lion told the jackal about his meeting with a strange-looking animal, like a goat, but who was not afraid of him at all. The jackal was very clever. He soon guessed that the cause of the lion's fear was only a poor old goat. He told the lion that it was the boldness of a weak old animal who didn't wish to be devoured.

"Come back with me to your cave, and make a meal of this pretender", he suggested.

The lion returned with the jackal. When the goat saw the lion returning, she understood everything, but she did not lose her courage. She walked towards them and said to the jackal, "Is this the way you carry out my orders? I sent you to get me ten lions to eat at once, and you have brought me only one!"

As soon as the lion heard this, he thought he had been betrayed by the jackal. He fell on him and tore him to pieces.

Seeing this, the goat walked out of the cave and ran away as quickly as she could.

Moral : One can escape from tricky situations with their wits and intelligence.

71. The Monkey and the Deer

Once a herd of deer lived by a lake. The grass was always green and there were no wild animals on their side of the lake. So they had a real good life. However their happiness did not last long. Once there was a severe draught and a great shortage of food. The lake got dried up and the place was no longer green. The deer were extremely sad and they started seeking advise from other animals to help them out of their misery. But no one was able to help them out.

Then they saw a monkey who seemed to be happy in his own world. The other animals warned the deer that the monkey was a foolish animal and they should not listen to him.

The deer ignored the animals and asked the monkey to help them out. The monkey told them about another lake that was on the other side of the forest. He told them that the lake was filled with water and the place was not impacted by draught.

The deer decided to migrate to this new place. When they reached the lake they were happy to find it exactly as described by the monkey. They started celebrating and did not notice a tiger watching them. The tiger saw his opportunity and leaped on the herd. After catching one deer, the tiger went away.

The remaining deer were sad to lose one of their friend and cursed themselves for acting on the monkey's advise in a haste.

Moral : Beware of an advise from a foolish person.

72. The Mouse, the Cat and the Dogs

Once there lived a little mouse in a forest. He was having a great time until a wild cat came to the forest. The cat was always chasing the mouse, trying to catch him. The mouse was extremely frustrated and he lost his sleep.

One day a hunter came to the forest accompanied with three dogs. The mouse devised a plan and secretly came out of his hiding place. He went to the three dogs and started dancing and mocking them. The three dogs were angry at the little mouse and leaped to catch him. The mouse was prepared and he ran towards the cat. As soon as the dogs saw the cat, they left the mouse and started to run towards her. The cat was shocked to see three dogs chasing her and she ran away with all her might, never to return back.

The mouse was happy to get rid of the cat.

Moral : An intelligent person can overcome any difficult situation.

73. The Lion and the Squirrel

There lived an arrogant and mean lion in a forest. He used to torture other animals. His terror was so widespread that all animals were scared of him and used to stay away from him. They reluctantly agreed to whatever the lion told them to do.

One day a little squirrel came to live in the forest. He saw the arrogant lion and decided to teach him a lesson.

The lion was resting under a tree. The squirrel crawled on his body and bit his nose. The irritated lion immediately got up. He found the little squirrel biting his nose. The lion roared, "How dare you bite me? I will kill you now."

The squirrel challenged, "Oh but before killing me, you must get me! I dare you to catch me!"

Saying so the squirrel ran away to the top of a tree. The lion chased the squirrel and crashed himself against the tree. Before he got a chance to recover, the squirrel came down at a lightning speed and struck the lion hard with its teeth. The lion writhed in pain and got a severe headache. He lost all his energy and gave up. He went back to his place cursing the little squirrel. The squirrel had indeed taught him a lesson.

Moral : Appearances are deceptive, a small person can also be a formidable foe.

74. The Farmer, his Son and the Donkey

A farmer and his son were once going with their donkey to market. As they were walking along by its side a countryman passed them and said: "You fools, what is a donkey for but to ride upon?"

So the farmer put the boy on the donkey and they went on their way. But soon they passed a group of men, one of whom said: "See that lazy youngster, he lets his father walk while he rides."

So the farmer ordered his son to get off, and got on himself. But they hadn't gone far when they passed two women, one of whom said to the other: "Shame on that lazy father to let his poor little son walk along."

Well, the farmer didn't know what to do, but at last he took his son up before him on the donkey. By this time they had come to the town, and the passers-by began to jeer and point at them. The farmer stopped and asked what they were scoffing at. The men said: "Aren't you ashamed of yourself for overloading that poor donkey of yours?"

The farmer and his son got off and tried to think what to do. They thought and they thought, till at last they cut down a pole, tied the donkey's feet to it, and raised the pole and the donkey to their shoulders. They went along amid the laughter of all who met them till they came to Market Bridge, when the donkey, getting one of his feet loose, kicked out and caused the boy to drop his end of the pole. In the struggle the donkey fell over the bridge, and his fore-feet being tied together he was drowned.

Moral : Please all and you will please none.

75. The Crow Couple and the Sea

Once, a crow and his wife were sitting near the sea. Suddenly, a big wave came and swept the crow's wife away. The crow cried and cried over the loss of his wife.

Soon, many crows gathered near him after hearing his cries. They asked him why he was crying. The crow told them everything. The crows felt very sad for the crow.

The crow decided to fast near the sea. He said, "I will not eat or sleep till I get my wife back."

Many days passed by but the crow did not give up his fasting. The sea-god was seeing all this. He felt pity for the crow and thought, 'He really does love his wife a lot.'

So impressed was the sea-god that he returned the crow's wife. The crow was very happy and thanked the sea-god.

Moral : True love is blessed by God.

76. The Ant and the Butterfly

On a pleasant summer day, a carefree butterfly was merrily dancing and singing. He had plenty to eat in this season. However, an ant was busy in carrying food. She was working hard to store food in her hole.

Seeing the ant working so hard, the butterfly mocked, "O poor ant! Why are you spoiling your days in collecting the food? You should have some fun. But you are silly working so hard!"

The ant replied calmly,"I'm not spoiling my days. I'm preparing myself for the harsh winter because it will not be the same then and I will not get any food. So I am preparing myself for the harsh adversity. Of course summer days are pleasant and enjoyable but we must also think about our future. I suggest that you should also prepare for the winter."

The butterfly ridiculed,"Ha, Ha, Ha! I'm not a fool like you to waste my happy days in storing the food."

Soon the pleasant summer days passed and the cold winter arrived. The flowers and plants dried up. With each passing day, it was becoming increasingly difficult to get any food.

The butterfly began starving, whereas the ant was having a nice time in her cozy home. She had enough to eat. The butterfly went to the ant for borrowing some food.

The ant said,"You fool! You spent the whole summer in dancing and singing. You did not think for the winter. Now you sing and dance in this winter as well. Go away from here! I will not help a lazy and short sighted person like you."

Moral : One should plan their time and resources wisely.

77. The Two Goats

There was a very narrow bridge on a river. Once two goats tried to cross this bridge from opposite sides. They started to argue with each other. Each of them wanted the other to back off so that it could pass. Each of them was proud and refused to give way to the other. Their argument soon turned into a violent fight and they locked their horns with each other.

They fought hard for some time and pushed each other down in the river where they got drowned.

Moral : False pride will lead to doom.

78. The Bird and the Farmer

There was a farmer who cultivated a land of paddy. There was a big tree on his farm on which there lived lot of birds. The birds used to eat small grains but they also used to protect the field by driving the pests away.

One season it did not rain as usual and there was a drought. The birds decided to ask the farmer for help. One bird went to the farmer and said, "Dear Farmer, please give us some food as we are hungry. We take care of your farm by driving away the pests."

But the farmer was a selfish man, he said, "Go away you pests. You are a nuisance to this farm!"

The farmer drove away all the birds.

The next season it rained properly and his land was very rich in paddy. The farmer thought that he would be very rich when he harvested his crops and sold it. But alas, one night the entire field was devastated by pests. The farmers realized his mistake too late.

Moral : Be grateful to people who help you.

79. The Grateful Monkey

Once there lived a poor old woman, in a village, with her grandson. Although she was poor, she doted on her grandson and tried to fulfill all his little wishes.

One day her grandson found a small monkey injured near a tree. He took the monkey to his home and took good care. Soon the monkey was completely cured. The old woman asked her grandson to send the monkey off to the forest as they could barely manage to survive and could not feed the monkey any longer. The grandson became sad and started crying.

The monkey saw the crying child and realized the situation. A couple of days before, he had seen some thieves hiding their stash under a tree. The monkey went to the old woman and pulled her sari. He dragged her to the place where the robbers had buried their treasure. After digging for some time, the old woman found a box filled with money and jewels. She thanked the monkey and took it back to her grandson. They lived happily ever after.

Moral : An act of kindness always has its rich rewards.

80. The Jackal and the Drum

There was once a jackal named Gomaya who was staying in a jungle.Once he set out in search of food and ended up at an abandoned battlefield whence he heard loud and strange sounds. Though scared, jackal decided to know the secret of these sounds.

Warily, the jackal marched in the direction of the sounds and found a drum there. It was this drum, which was sending the sounds whenever the branches of the tree above brushed against it.

Relieved, the jackal began playing the drum and thought that there could be food inside it. The jackal entered the drum by piercing its side. He was disappointed to find no food in it. Yet he consoled himself saying that he rid himself of the fear of sound.

Moral : Don't be afraid of false things.

81. The Rabbit and the Fox

One day a fox caught a rabbit and decided to carry it to his home and share it with his family. He put the rabbit in a sack and tied it's end with a string. Along the way, the fox was thirsty and he saw a pond. He kept the sack aside on the meadow and went to drink water.

The rabbit struggled for a while and finally managed to escape from the sack. He thought that if the fox feels an empty sack he will again chase and catch him. So he got a big rock and dropped it in the sack and again tied its end with the string. Then the rabbit ran away.

The fox returned back after some time and took the sack on his back. Due to the weight of the rock, the fox never guessed that the rabbit had already escaped. The fox gave the sack to his wife who was also hungry.

The fox said, "Dear, the rabbit inside the sack is very cunning. He will surely escape if we open the sack, so let us just put the entire sack in the boiling water and then after it is cooked, we can have a good meal."

The wife agreed and she kept a pot of water to boil. After some time, the water started boiling and the fox dropped the sack inside the pot. But alas! due to the rock the pot tumbled and all the boiling water spilled on the fox and his wife. The fox burnt his skin and decided that he will never again catch a rabbit.

Moral : You can defeat a strong enemy with your wits and intelligence.

82. Hello Cave!

Long ago, there lived a lion by the name of Kharanakhara. He had been trying to hunt for his prey for the last two days, but could not succeed due to his old age and physical infirmity. He was no longer strong to hunt for his food. He was quite dejected and disappointed. He thought that he would die of starving. One day, while he was wandering in the jungle hopelessly, he came across a cave. 'There must be some animal who lives in this cave'; so thought the lion. 'I will hide myself inside it and wait for its occupant to enter. And as soon as the occupant enters the cave, I shall kill him and eat his flesh.' Thinking thus, the lion entered the cave and hid himself carefully. After sometime, a fox came near the cave. The cave belonged to her. The fox was surprised to find the foot-marks of a lion pointing towards the cave. 'Some lion has stealthily entered my cave', she thought to herself. But to make sure of the presence of the lion inside the cave, the fox played upon a trick.

The fox stood at some distance from the cave to save herself in case of a sudden attack and shouted, "Hello cave! I've come back. Speak to me as you have been doing earlier. Why're you keeping silent, my dear cave? May I come in and occupy my residence?"

Hearing the fox calling the cave, the lion thought to himself, that the cave he was hiding in, must in reality be a talking cave. The cave might be keeping quiet because of his kingly presence inside. Therefore, if the cave didn't answer to the fox's question, the fox might go away to occupy some other cave and thus, he would have to go without a meal once again.

Trying to be wise, the lion answered in a roaring voice on behalf of the cave, "I've not forgotten my practice of speaking to you when you come, my dear fox. Come in and be at home, please."

Thus, the clever fox confirmed the presence of the lion hiding in her cave and ran away without losing a single moment, saying, "Only a fool would believe that a cave speaks."

Moral : Presence of mind is the best weapon to guard oneself.

83. The Rabbit and the Jackal

Once a young rabbit and a jackal were good friends. All the other rabbits warned the young rabbit to stay away from the sly jackal, but he never listened to them. The jackal was indeed very cunning and waited for an opportunity to make the young rabbit his prey. The sly jackal won the young rabbit's trust and one day, invited him for dinner.

The young rabbit did not sense any foul play and accepted the invitation.

The jackal and his wife made the dinner table ready. The jackal cooked only some soup, so his wife asked, "Dear, you have invited your friend, the rabbit, for dinner. But why have you cooked only soup? You could have had a feast with many dishes."

"No my dear! We will indeed have a feast as we will be eating the rabbit itself for dinner today. I have added sleeping pills in this soup. Once the rabbit comes, I will ask him to drink this soup and when he becomes unconscious, we can make him our prey and have our grand feast", explained the jackal.

But the jackal did not knew that the rabbit had already arrived and had listened to his conversation. The rabbit felt sad for ignoring his elders advice, but devised a clever plan.

As soon as the jackal asked him to drink the soup, the rabbit said, "Dear jackal, it will be bad manners to eat before my elders. You and your wife, both, are elder to me, so please have the soup first and then I will have it."

The jackal and his wife were scared to drink the soup and they spilled it. As soon as the young rabbit saw it, he quickly ran away and saved his life.

Moral : Stay away from your natural enemy.

84. The Fat Fox

Once the animals in the forest decided to have a wrestling match. The giraffe was appointed as the referee and the judge. All the mighty animals such as lion, tiger and elephant participated in the contest.

A young fox wanted to be a wrestler and went to the giraffe. The giraffe scolded, "Fox, you are very lean and the other mighty animals will kill you. Get lost from here!"

The disappointed fox wanted to get fat quickly so that he too could participate in the contest. He went to a monkey who advised him to drink honey to become fat quickly. The monkey played a prank, but the innocent fox believed him.

The young fox went to a big tree and saw a beehive. He threw some rocks at the hive, hoping that it will fall down and then he can drink the honey. But alas! all the honey bee's attacked and bit him. The fox managed to somehow save himself and went to the contest arena.

His body was swollen due to the bites and he appeared to have grown fat. The giraffe was amazed to see the fox and asked, "How did you get fat so quickly?"

But the fox could not speak as he was still in pain. The sly monkey laughed and said, "Judge Giraffe! This is not fat but the gift from the honey-bees."

The fox regretted for listening to the foolish advise of the monkey.

Moral : Never take a fool's advise seriously.

85. The Language of Animals

Ranga was a farmer who was living happily in his small village. He had few hens, a cow and a dog and he was kind to all the animals. One day a famous Swami visited the village for a sermon. Ranga took good care of the Swami and pleased him. While leaving the village, Swamiji told Ranga to ask for any boon.

After thinking for a while, Ranga said, "Swamiji, Please give me a boon so that I can understand the language of all animals and birds."

The Swami was surprised at this strange request and said, "Dear Ranga, this knowledge cannot be of any use. But since I promised you, I grant you the wish. You will be able to understand the language of all animals after you get up tomorrow morning."

Next day, Ranga got up excitedly and went to the hen-coop. The hen had not laid any egg so he asked, "Where are the eggs hen?"

"Can't you wait for sometime? Go away and don't bother me", yelled the angry hen.

Ranga was scared and he went inside the house. After his lunch, he kept the left-overs in a dish for the dog. The dog came inside and growled, "Ranga, you eat nice hot and fresh meal everyday and keep the cold left-overs for me. You must give me fresh hot cooked meal going forward else I will bite you."

The terrified Ranga promised to serve fresh food to his dog.

Later at night, Ranga went inside his room and slept on his bed. Suddenly the door opened and the cow came inside the bedroom. Ranga asked the cow, "Why did you come inside?"

"I am cold outside and I will sleep here in this cozy warm room from now onwards. If you resist, I will kill you with my sharp horns," warned the cow.

Poor Ranga ran away and went in search of the Swamiji. He soon found the Swami and fell at his feet. "Swami, please take back your boon as it has become a curse for me. I am sorry that I did not listen to your advise earlier."

The Swamiji took pity on Ranga and took back the boon. Ranga was back to his normal self.

Moral : A foolish desire can cause harm.

86. The Monkey and the King

Once there was a king, who had a pet monkey. This monkey was a fool, but was treated royally and moved freely in the king's palace. He was also allowed to enter the king's personal rooms that were forbidden even for the confidential servants.

One afternoon, the king was asleep, while the monkey kept a watch. All of a sudden, a fly came in the room and sat on the king's nose. The monkey swayed her away, but the fly would only go away for some time and return on the king's nose again. The monkey got very angry and excited. The foolish monkey started chasing the fly with a sword.

As the fly sat on the king's nose again, the monkey hit the fly with all his might. The fly flew away unharmed, but the king was severely wounded and lost his nose.

Moral : Beware of a foolish friend. He can cause you more harm than your enemy.

87. The Rabbit who Fooled the Fox

Once a starving fox was searching for food when he saw a rabbit on the other side of the bushes. The rabbit too saw the fox. The fox knew that he will not be able to catch the rabbit as he was very tired. So the fox decided to play a trick. He suddenly growled and fell down pretending to be dead. He laid there motionless.

The rabbit thought that the fox was dead and went near to verify. But as soon as he got near, the fox pounced and caught him. The fox was about to gulp the rabbit when the rabbit started shouting, "Run, run, I see a lion coming here!"

The fox got scared and ran away leaving the rabbit behind. There was no lion as the rabbit had fooled the fox and saved himself.

Moral : Tit for Tat

88. Who is Great?

One day an argument broke out between a cat and an elephant on who was more courageous. The elephant said, "Look at me! I am huge and obviously more courageous than you are."

The cat said, "You might be big, but I am more courageous. I can prove it, follow me."

The elephant followed the cat to a big tree. A small mouse lived in the hollow of the tree. The mouse was playing when it saw the elephant. The mouse did not care the elephant's presence and continued playing. Then suddenly the cat said "meow". As soon as the mouse heard the "meow" of the cat, it got terrified and ran inside the trunk of the elephant.

The cat explained, "Dear elephant, you saw that the little mouse was not scared of you but when he just heard my voice, he ran away. This proves that I am more courageous than you are."

But the elephant was irritated by the mouse in its trunk and sneezed loudly. The sound of the sneeze scared the cat away. When the little mouse saw that the cat had gone away, he came out and walked away. The elephant thought, "Neither me, nor the cat are courageous. It is this little mouse who is more courageous than both of us."

Moral : Courage is not determined by the size of a person.

89. The Stag and His Antlers

It is a known fact that Stags have beautiful antlers. The Stags are proud of their branched out antlers.

Once, a stag was enjoying the beauty of his antlers on seeing his reflections in the pond water.

He thought, "What beautiful antlers I have! They are the most beautiful of all."

The stag looked down at his legs and got so sad. He once again said to himself, "Look at my legs! They are so lean and bony. They are the ugliest of all."

At that moment, he heard the growl of a tiger. He started running. His legs took him fast away from the tiger.

But what a pity his antlers got entwined with a bush of thorns and would not get free.

The stag tried hard to get the antlers free, but in vain. At last, he began to kick front and back, and what a surprise, the Stag got free.

Now, his thoughts have changed.

Moral : Mere beauty without utility is of no value.

90. The Three Sparrows

One there lived three sparrows who were friends. One day, the elder sparrow said to the other two, "Friends, soon it will be rainy season. We each must build a strong house for ourself to protect us from the rain and the wind."

They all agreed. The youngest sparrow was lazy and she kept postponing the task. The second sparrow was a miser and she spent less money and built a house with just a few dry leaves and twigs. The eldest sparrow was wise, she worked hard and built a sturdy house for herself.

Soon the rains started and it rained very heavily one day. The first sparrow, did not have a shelter and went to the second sparrow. But the second sparrow lamented, "Friend! The rains washed my house and I, too, have no place to live."

They both, then, went to the third sparrow who welcomed them. She said, "Friends, I hope you have now realized that we should always plan ourselves for our future."

The other two sparrows agreed and promised to be careful in future.

Moral : We must plan for our future carefully.

91. The Dog and the Old Woman

Leela was an old woman who lived alone in a village. After her husband's death a few weeks back, she stayed all alone in her big house. She was worried that thieves might come and loot her. So she went to her neighbor Raghu and asked for help. Raghu gave his dog to her and said, "Leelaji, don't worry. This dog will protect you."

Leela thanked him and took the dog with her. She took good care of the dog and they became friends soon. Here, Raghu had other plans. He always eyed on Leela's wealth and wanted to steal it. That was the reason he gave his own dog to Leela, so that the dog will not bite him when he goes to steal there.

One night, when he saw that Leela had gone for sleep, he quietly went inside her house to steal. But the dog got up and started barking loudly. The dog also bit Raghu and wounded him. Leela woke up and was shocked to see Raghu trying to steal from her. She said, "Shame on you Raghu. I trusted you, but your dog is more loyal than you."

The king's guards came and took Raghu away.

Moral : An animal is more loyal than a human.

92. The Bear, the Rabbit and the Monkey

One day a rabbit was strolling happily by the river when he suddenly came across a big bear. The bear was happy to see its prey. But suddenly a monkey came there and said, "O rabbit! do not be afraid of this bear. He looks big but he has no strength and he cannot harm you."

"How dare you monkey? I will now not only have the rabbit but also will make you my lunch," retorted the angry bear.

"O bear! I dare you to shake this big tree. If you can do it, I will be happy to become your lunch", said the monkey pointing to a tree by the river.

The bear accepted and the three of them went to the tree. The bear started shaking the tree wildly.It was a coconut tree and due to the violent shaking, all the coconut fell down on the bear's head and he fell down unconscious. The monkey saved the life of the rabbit and they both ran away.

Moral : Intelligence and wits are more powerful than physical strength.

93. The Rooster, the Cat and the Mouse

One day a little mouse decided to go out alone and explore the outside world. Thus the inexperienced little mouse set off on a journey.

After a while, he came across a rooster. Never having seen one before, the little mouse was so scared of the rooster's beak, its feathers and red crest, that he ran off as fast as he could.

Further on, the mouse saw a cat. "What a good-looking and handsome animal", he thought, "with a soft fur and lovely striking eyes!"

When the mouse got back home, he told his mother what he had seen.

The mother was shocked.

"You silly mouse," the mother said, "Never go by external appearances. The terrible animal that you saw was a harmless rooster, while the fine looking one is our mortal enemy, the cat".

Moral : One should not form opinions just by outer appearance.

94. The Pigeon's Verdict

Once a crow and a sparrow decided to plant an apple tree. The sparrow got the seeds and said to crow, "Let us go and plant these seeds."

But the lazy crow excused himself saying, "I am having cold, can you please go alone and plant the seeds."

The sparrow went and planted the seeds. Then after some days the sparrow again said, "Friend, let us go and water our tree."

The lazy crow again excused himself, "I have a headache, can you please do it alone."

So alone she went and watered the tree. This repeated often and the sparrow alone took care of the tree because each time the crow had a new excuse. Finally apples grew on the tree and the sparrow said, "Friend, let us go and share the apples."

The crow agreed and they both went to the tree. The sparrow had already created five equal stacks, she said, "Friend, three stacks for me and two for you."

But the crow did not agree, "No, no, the tree belongs to both of us and I must get an equal share."

They fought and finally decided to go to the judge pigeon. Judge pigeon heard the stories from both the sides and finally passed the verdict. He said, "It is a fact that the sparrow alone worked hard on the tree and the lazy crow did not help on any task. Hence the entire share of apples belong only to the sparrow and the crow should not get anything."

The crow cursed himself for his laziness.

Moral : Hard work alone pays.

95. The King of Rat's

One day the king of rat's wanted to see how a human king lives. So he went to king Veerendra's palace and was looking around. Suddenly a cat saw the rat king and pounced to catch him. The rat king managed to escape and went to Veerendra's bedroom. The cat followed the rat king. King Veerendra was sleeping and the rat king sneaked inside his pillow. Veerendra got up and took out his sword.

"Who dares to disturb me? I will kill you now", he said raising his sword.

The rat king pleaded, "Dear king, I am also the king of rats and I just came her to see how you live. Please spare my life now and I will return back the favor by helping you in your hour of need in future."

The king laughed but he spared the rat king out of pity.

After some days the neighbor king Ravindra attacked Veerendra's kingdom. King Veerendra was caught off guard and he was not prepared. The news reached the rat king and he decided to pay back the earlier favor.

At night, the rat king with his fellow rats went to the enemy camp of king Ravindra and bit all the bows, arrows, clothes and other armor. They destroyed many weapons and war equipment. Next day king Ravindra was shocked to see the status of his army. When king Veerendra knew about it, he and his men fought hard and won the war. King Veerendra then went to the rat king and thanked him for his help.

Moral : Hard work alone pays.

96. The Foolish Fox

One day a fox saw a rabbit and pounced at it. The rabbit had no chance to escape, so he devised a plan. He started shivering and laughing loudly. The fox was surprised and asked him the reason for the change in his behavior.

The rabbit said, in a loud voice, "I am a demon and have possessed this rabbit. But his body is so small. I am now happy that you will eat him and then I can possess you and live in your big body. I will be much more comfortable."

As soon as he heard the "demon", the terrified fox ran away without even looking back. The clever rabbit saved his life with his wits.

Moral : A foolish person can believe any tale.

97. The Scorpion's Revenge

There was a hollow in the bark of a big tree in the forrest. The crabs used to live in this hollow. Once a fox came to the forrest and saw the crabs. He thought of a plan. Everyday he used to put his tail in the hollow, and the younger crabs would catch it thinking it as a toy. The fox would then run away and eat the crab stuck to its tail. This continued for many days and the crabs were worried about their young ones. They called a meeting and decided to take help from their friend, the scorpion. The scorpion heard their story and was moved with pity. He decided to help the crabs.

Next day scorpion went into one hollow and waited for the fox. As usual the fox came and put his tail in the hollow. As soon as the scorpion saw the tail, it bit it hard with all its might. The fox screamed in pain and ran away. He never dared to return back to the tree. All the crabs thanked the scorpion for helping them.

Moral : An Evil person always meets his end in a painful way.

98. The Red Stone Ring

Once a deer found a red stone ring near a big tree in the forrest. He liked the ring a lot and took it. He considered the ring to be his lucky charm and tied it to its antler.

One day a fox saw the ring and wished to have it. But the deer would not give the ring. So one day when the deer was sleeping, the fox came silently and stole away the ring. A monkey on the tree saw this and told the deer when he woke up.

The deer confronted the fox but he denied stealing the ring. The deer went away disappointed. On his way he decided to take the help of his friend, the giraffe. The giraffe devised a plan to get back the stolen ring.

He went around the forrest announcing that the lion king had lost his red stone ring and warned that the thief would be severely punished. The giraffe made sure that the fox heard his announcement.

The fox got scared and returned the ring back to the deer. On his way back he saw the lion. So to impress the lion, the fox said, "Your Majesty! I think the deer is the thief of your ring. I saw the ring with him."

The lion was surprised and did not knew what the fox was talking about. He said, "I think you have gone mad fox. I do not care for any ring, but I am starving and now that you are here, I think I have got my meal."

Saying so he pounced on the fox and killed him.

Moral : Evil acts never go unpunished.

99. The Cobra and the Ants

There lived a big king cobra in a dense forest. As usual, he fed on birds' eggs, lizards, frogs and other small creatures. The whole night he hunted the small creatures and when the day broke, he went into his hole to sleep. Gradually, he became fat. And his fat grew to such a measure that it became difficult for him to enter and come out of his hole without being scratched.

Ultimately, he decided to abandon his hole and selected a huge tree for his new home. But there was an ant hill at the root of the tree. It was impossible for king cobra to put up with the ants. So, he went to the ant hill and said, "I'm King Cobra, the king of this forest. I order all of you to go from this place and live somewhere else."

There were other animals, too, around. They began trembling with fear to see such a huge snake before them. They ran for their lives. But the ants paid no heed to his threats. Thousands of ants streamed out of the ant hill. Soon they were swarming all over the body of the king cobra, stinging and biting him. Thousands of thorny pricks all over his body caused unbearable pain to him. The king cobra tried to keep the ants away, but in vain. He wriggled in pain and died at last.

Moral : Sometimes even a small person can be a formidable foe.

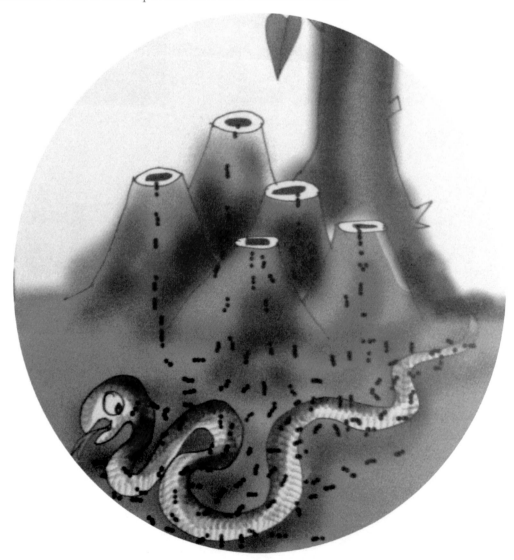

100. True Friends

Once there were four friends, a crow, a hen, a duck and a tortoise. The duck and the tortoise lived in a river. They always told stories about the various animals and other fancy things in the water. The crow and the hen were amused by these stories and they wished they too could swim. One day the tortoise and the duck found them in dull spirits, so they asked, "Friends, why are you so dull? Please tell us."

The crow and the hen said, "Friends, we always hear stories from you about the river and we too wish to go in the water. But we are sad because we cannot swim."

The duck and the tortoise thought for a while and devised a plan, they said, "Friends, you need not worry. We can take you in the water"

"But how?", asked the curious crow and the hen in chorus.

"The crow can ride on my back", said the tortoise.

"And the hen can ride on my back", said the duck.

So the crow rode on the tortoise's back and the hen on the duck's back. All other animals saw this scene with much amazement. The friends helped each other to fulfill their desires.

Moral : A friend in need is a friend indeed.

101. The Clever Rabbit

There lived a lion by the name of Bhasuraka, in a dense jungle. He was very powerful, cruel and arrogant. He used to kill the animals of the jungle unnecessarily. He even killed the human beings, who travelled through the jungle. This became a cause of worry for all the animals. They discussed this problem amongst themselves and ultimately came upon a decision to hold a meeting with the lion and make an amicable settlement with him and put an end to this ongoing trauma.

So, one day, all the animals of the jungle assembled under a big tree. They also invited king lion to attend the meeting. In the meeting the animals said to king lion, "Your Majesty, we are happy that you are our king. We are all-the-more happy that you are presiding over the meeting."

King lion thanked them and asked, "Why is it that we have gathered here?" All the animal began looking at each other. They had to muster enough courage to broach the topic. "Sir," said one of the animals, "Its natural that you kill us for food. But, killing more than what is required is a positive vice and unnecessary. If you go on killing the animals without any purpose, soon a day will come, when there will be no animals left in the jungle."

"So what do you want?" roared king lion.

"Your Majesty, we have already discussed the problem among ourselves and have come upon a solution. We have decided to send one animal a day to your den. You can kill and eat it. This will save you from the trouble of hunting and you will not have to kill a number of animals unnecessarily for your meals."

"Good," the lion roared back. "I agree to this proposal, but the animals must reach to me on time, otherwise, I'll kill all the animals of the jungle." The animals agreed to this proposal.

Everyday one animal walked into the lion's den to become his feast. The lion too was very happy to have his food right before him. He stopped hunting for his prey.

One day, it was the turn of a hare to go into the lion's den. The little hare was unwilling to go and become a meal of the lion, but the other animals forced him to go to the lion's den.Having no alternative, the hare began thinking quickly. He thought of a plan. He began wandering around and made a deliberate delay, and reached the lion's den little later than the lion's meal time. By now, the lion had already lost his patience and seeing the hare coming slowly, he became furious and demanded for an explanation.

"Your Majesty", the hare said with folded hands, "I am not to be blamed for that. I have come late because another lion began chasing me and wanted to eat me. He said that he too was the king of the jungle."

The king lion roared in great anger and said, "Impossible, there cannot exist another king in this jungle. Who is he? I'll kill him. Show me where he lives."

The lion and the hare set out to face the other lion. The hare took the lion to a deep well, full of water.

When they reached near the well, the hare said to the lion, "This is the place where he lives. He might be hiding inside."

The lion again roared in great anger; climbed up the well and peeped in. He saw his own reflection in the water and thought that the other lion was challenging his authority. He lost his temper.

"I must kill him", said the lion unto himself and jumped into the well. He was soon drowned.

The hare was happy. He went back to other animals and narrated the whole story. All the animals took a sigh of relief and praised him for his cleverness. They all lived happily thereafter.

Moral : Intelligence is superior to physical strength.

If you liked this book, you might also enjoy our other books, Search for "Vyanst" on Amazon:-

1) Mahabharat for Children – Parts 1 & 2 (Illustrated)

ASIN: - B00SSOYG2W

2) Prince Dhruv, Bhakta Prahlad & Other valiant Heroes (Illustrated)

ASIN: - B00TU965V0

3) Sri Krishna Leela for Children (Illustrated)

ASIN: - B00TWOE6DM

4) Dashavatar Tales for Children – The 10 Avatars of Lord Vishnu (Illustrated)

ASIN: - B00UATSNCI

5) Good Karma – Moral stories for children (Illustrated)

ASIN: - B00UEH9EQK

6) Virtues and Values – Shrawan Kumar and other Moral stories for children (Illustrated)

ASIN: - B00UDFQJYS

7) Panchatantra 51 short stories with Moral (Illustrated)

ASIN: - B00B73O7RQ

8) Panchatantra 40 More Stories with Moral (Illustrated)

ASIN: - B00B7OICDU

9) Jataka Tales 51 Short Stories with Moral (Illustrated)

ASIN: - B00OTK408A

10) 51 Animal Tales with Moral (Illustrated) – Folktales from India

ASIN: - B00SSOYG2W

11) Festivals of India Part 1 – 51 Hindu Festivals & Fairs (Illustrated)

ASIN: - B00RC1CYBI

12) Festivals of India Part 2 – Sikh, Jain, Buddhist, Parsi, Sindhi & Other festivals

ASIN: - B00RPOSIZ8

13) Paramananda and his foolish disciples (With Pictures)

ASIN: - B00SBEZLII

14) 51 Moral Stories, Folk Tales from India (Illustrated)

ASIN: - B00TSI2NFK

15) Wits of Mulla Nasruddin: Stories based on Indian folklore (Illustrated)

ASIN: - B00YDCSRG0

16) The two brothers & magic mangoes: Based on a folk story from South India (Illustrated)

ASIN: - B00WEL9JMI

17) Doha's – Stories for children based on Famous couplets of Tulsidas, Kabir & Rahim

ASIN: - B00Y5FLUZ0

18) Choturam & Pandit Vaidyanath – The tales of Bodhisattva (Illustrated)

ASIN: - B00WFPQLDI

19) Ramayana for children (Illustrated)

ASIN: - B00W6KVVBE

20) Ashtavinayak & other lord Ganesha stories (Illustrated)

ASIN: - B00UKB8UCE

21) Ganga, Shakuntala & Damayanti – Valiant Heroines from Hindu Mythology (Illustrated)

ASIN: - B00Y1BEMOE

22) Stories of Hindu Goddess Durga (Illustrated)

ASIN: - B00WPWQ2VC

23) 31 More Animal Tales with Moral: Folk tales from India (Illustrated)

ASIN: - B00WKV0KWA

24) The inimitable Birbal : Stories of wit and humor (Illustrated)

ASIN: - B00YGHQFOI

25) Maryada Ramanna: Stories of wits and wisdom (Illustrated)

ASIN: - B00YK8A7V0

26) All in one Humor Omnibus: Tales of Birbal, Tenali Rama, Mulla Nasruddin, Maryada Raman & Paramananda (Illustrated)

ASIN: - B00YY9YIS8

27) The Magic Horse and Other Tales: Stories based on Arabian nights (Illustrated)

ASIN: - B00ZDC9O20

We welcome your feedback / comments / suggestions. Our email i.d. :-

VYANST@GMAIL.COM

THE END

Made in the USA
San Bernardino, CA
27 June 2016